dup.

MVFOL

D0090204

A CHILDREN'S BIBLE

A CHILDREN'S BIBLE

———

A NOVEL

LYDIA MILLET

W. W. NORTON & COMPANY

Independent Publishers Since 1923

For information about permission to reproduce selections from this book, write to Permissions, W. W. Norton & Company, Inc., 500 Fifth Avenue, New York, NY 10110

For information about special discounts for bulk purchases, please contact W. W. Norton Special Sales at specialsales@wwnorton.com or 800-233-4830

Manufacturing by Lake Book Manufacturing
Production manager: Julia Druskin

Library of Congress Cataloging-in-Publication Data

Names: Millet, Lydia, 1968– author.
Title: A children's bible : a novel / Lydia Millet.
Description: First edition. | New York, NY : W. W. Norton & Company, [2020]
Identifiers: LCCN 2019050471 | ISBN 9781324005032 (hardcover) | ISBN 9781324005049 (epub)
Classification: LCC PS3563.I42175 C48 2020 | DDC 813/.54—dc23
LC record available at https://lccn.loc.gov/2019050471

W. W. Norton & Company, Inc., 500 Fifth Avenue, New York, N.Y. 10110
www.wwnorton.com

W. W. Norton & Company Ltd., 15 Carlisle Street, London W1D 3BS

1 2 3 4 5 6 7 8 9 0

A CHILDREN'S BIBLE

1

ONCE WE LIVED in a summer country. In the woods there were treehouses, and on the lake there were boats.

Even the smallest canoe could take us down to the ocean. We'd paddle across the lake, over a marsh, down a stream, and come to the river's mouth. Where the water met the sky. We'd run along the beach on a salt breeze, leaving our boats on the sand.

We found the skull of a dinosaur. Or maybe a porpoise. We found skate eggs and shark-eye shells and sea glass.

Before sunset we'd paddle back to the lake, returning for dinner. Loons sent their haunting calls across the water. To wash the sand from our ankles, we jumped off the dock. And screamed. We dove and flipped as the sky turned violet.

Uphill from the dock, deer ambled onto the sweeping lawn.

Their grace was deceptive, though: they carried ticks, and ticks carried disease. It could make you crazy, steal your memories, swell your legs. Or droop your face like a basset hound's.

So when they bent their elegant necks to nibble the grass, some of us shouted taunts. Sprinted toward them, flailing.

Some of us enjoyed seeing them panic. They'd bolt in a high-kicking flight toward the trees, frightened by our power. Some of us cheered as the deer fled.

Not me. I kept silent. I was sorry for them. The ticks weren't their fault.

To a deer, people were probably monsters. Certain people, anyway. At times, when a deer saw a man walking in the forest, he might prick up his ears and stand still as a statue. Waiting. Wary. Meaning no harm.

What are you? asked his ears. And oh. What am I?

Sometimes the answer was, You're dead.

And the deer crumpled to his knees.

A FEW PETS had come with us for the summer: three dogs and a cat, a pissed-off Siamese with a skin condition. Dandruff. We dressed up the dogs in costumes from a wicker chest, but could not dress the cat. She scratched.

One dog got makeup applied to its face, lipstick and blue eye shadow. It was a white-faced dog, so the makeup showed up well. We liked to have an impact. When we were done, the lipstick went back into some mother's Fendi handbag. We watched her apply it, unaware. That was satisfying.

We put the dogs in a play and invited the parents, since there was no one else to be an audience. But the pets were poorly trained and failed to take direction. There were two soldiers and a fancy lady we'd dressed in a frilly padded bra. The soldiers were cowards. Deserters, basically. They ran away when we issued the battle cry. (A blaring klaxon. It went *hoh-onk*.)

The lady urinated.

"Oh, poor old thing, she has a *nervous bladder*!" exclaimed someone's chubby mother. "Is that a *Persian* rug?"

Whose mother was it? Unclear. No one would cop to it, of course. We canceled the performance.

"Admit it, that was *your* mother," said a kid named Rafe to a kid named Sukey, when the parents had filed out. Some of their goblets, highball glasses, and beer bottles were completely empty. Drained.

Those parents were in a hurry, then.

"No way," said Sukey firmly, and shook her head.

"Then who *is* your mother? The one with the big ass? Or the one with the clubfoot?"

"Neither," said Sukey. "So fuck you."

THE GREAT HOUSE had been built by robber barons in the nineteenth century, a palatial retreat for the green months. Our parents, those so-called figures of authority, roamed its rooms in vague circuits beneath the broad beams, their objectives murky. And of no general interest.

They liked to drink: it was their hobby, or—said one of

us—maybe a form of worship. They drank wine and beer and whiskey and gin. Also tequila, rum, and vodka. At midday they called it the hair of the dog. It seemed to keep them contented. Or going, at least. In the evenings they assembled to eat food and drink more.

Dinner was the only meal we had to attend, and even that we resented. They sat us down and talked about nothing. They aimed their conversation like a dull gray beam. It hit us and lulled us into a stupor. What they said was so boring it filled us with frustration, and after more minutes, rage.

Didn't they know there were urgent subjects? Questions that needed to be asked?

If one of us said something serious, they dismissed it.

MayIpleasebeexcused.

Later the talk grew louder. Freed of our influence, some of them emitted sudden, harsh barks. Apparently, laughing. From the wraparound porch, with its bamboo torches and hanging ferns and porch swings, moth-eaten armchairs and blue-light bug zappers, the barks of laughter carried. We heard them from the treehouses and tennis courts and from the field of beehives a slow neighbor woman tended in the daytime, muttering under the veil of her beekeeping hat. We heard them from behind the cracked panes of the dilapidated greenhouse or on the cool black water of the lake, where we floated in our underwear at midnight.

I liked to prowl the moonlit grounds by myself with a flashlight, bouncing its spot over walls with white-shuttered windows, bicycles left lying on the grass, cars sitting quiet

on the wide crescent drive. When I came into earshot of the
laughter, I'd wonder that any of them could actually have
said something funny.

As the evenings wore on, some parents got it into their
heads to dance. A flash of life would move their lumpen
bodies. Sad spectacle. They flopped, blasting their old-time
music. "Beat on the brat, beat on the brat, beat on the brat
with a baseball bat, oh yeah."

The ones with no flashes of life sat in their chairs watching the dancers. Slack-faced, listless—for practical purposes,
deceased.

But less embarrassing.

Some parents paired off and crept into the second-floor
bedrooms, where a few boys among our number spied on
them from between the slats of closet doors. Saw them per-
form their dark acts.

At times they felt stirrings. I knew this. Although they
did not admit it.

More often, repugnance.

Most of us were headed to junior or senior year after the
summer was over, but a few hadn't even hit puberty—there
was a range of ages. In short, some were innocents. Others
performed dark acts of their own.

Those were not as repugnant.

HIDING OUR PARENTAGE was a leisure pursuit, but one we
took seriously. Sometimes a parent would edge near, threat-

ening to expose us. Risking the revelation of a family bond. Then we ran like rabbits.

We had to hide the running, though, in case our haste betrayed us, so truer to say we slipped out quietly. When one of *my* parents appeared, my technique was: pretend to catch sight of someone in the next room. Move in a natural manner toward this figment of my imagination, making a purposeful face. Go through the door. And fade away.

The first week of our stay, in early June, several parents had mounted the stairs to the rambling attic where we slept, some of us on bunk beds but more of us on the floor. We heard their voices calling out to the youngest. "Coming to tuck you *i-in!*"

We hid under our covers, blankets pulled over our heads, and some of us yelled rudely. The parents retreated, possibly offended. A sign went up on the door, PARENT FREE ZONE, and we spoke to them sternly in the morning.

"You have the run of the mansion," said Terry, calmly but forcefully. "Your own private bedrooms. Your own private attached baths."

He wore glasses and was squat and very pretentious. Still, he looked commanding as he stood there, his short arms crossed, at the head of the table.

The parents sipped their coffee. It made sucking noises.

"We have *one* room. For all of us. *One single room!*" intoned Terry. "For pity's sake. Give us our blessed space. In that minuscule scrap of territory. Think of the attic as a reservation. Imagine you're the white conquerors who brutally massacred our people. And we're the Indians."

"Native *Americans*," said a mother.

"Insensitive metaphor," said another. "Culturally."

"ONE OF THE mothers has a clubfoot?" asked Jen. "Huh. I never noticed."

"What *is* a clubfoot?" asked Low.

His name was actually Lorenzo, but that was too long, plus he was the tallest one of all of us, so we called him Low. Rafe had coined it. Low didn't mind.

"It drags," said Rafe. "That shoe with a thick heel. You know? That fat one's Sukey's mother, I bet."

"Sure, sure. Is *not*," said Sukey. "My mother's *way* better than that shit. My mother could kick that mother's ass."

"It can't be no one's mother," objected Low.

"Well. It *could*," said Sukey.

"There *are* some single ones," pointed out Juicy. He was called that because of his saliva, which was plentiful. He liked to spit.

"And childless couples," said Jen. "Sadly, barren."

"Destined to die without issue," added Terry, who fancied himself a wordsmith. His real name was Something the Third. As if that wasn't bad enough, "the Third" translated to "Tertius" in Latin. Then "Tertius" shortened to "Terry." So obviously that was what they called him.

He kept a private journal in which his feelings were recorded, possibly. The possibility was widely mocked.

"Yeah, but I saw the fat one in the kitchen groping Sukey's father," said Rafe.

"Untrue," said Sukey. "My father's dead."

"Been dead for years," nodded Jen.

"And still dead now," said David.

"Stepfather, then. What*ever*," said Rafe.

"They're not married."

"A technicality."

"I saw them too," said Low. "She had her hand right on his pants. The package. Right *on* there. Guy had a raging boner."

"Gross," said Juicy. He spat.

"God*damm*it, Juice. You almost hit my toe," said Low. "Demerit."

"Your fault for wearing *sandals*," said Juicy. "Mega lame. A demerit to *you*."

We had a system of accounting, a chart on a wall. There were merits and demerits. A merit was for an outrage successfully committed, a demerit for an act that should bring on humiliation. Juicy got merits for drooling into cocktails undetected, while Low got demerits for kissing up to a father. Probably not his own—Low's parentage was a well-kept secret. But he'd been spotted asking a guy with male-pattern baldness for wardrobe advice.

Low was a baby-faced giant of Mongolian descent, adopted from Kazakhstan. He was the worst dresser among us, rocking a seventies look that involved tie-dyed tank tops and short-shorts with white piping. Some made of terrycloth.

WE WOULDN'T HAVE been able to keep the parent game going if not for the parents' near-total disinterest. They had a hands-off attitude. "Where's Alycia?" I heard a mother say.

Alycia was the oldest of us, seventeen. And already a freshman in college.

"I've barely seen her since we got here," went on the voice. "What is it, two weeks now?"

The mother was speaking from the breakfast room, out of my field of view. I liked that room a lot, with its long, oaken table and glass walls on three sides. You could see the bright sparkle of the lake through the glass walls, and sunlight shifted through the moving branches of an ancient willow that shaded the house.

But the room was teeming with parents every morning. We couldn't use it.

I tried for a voice ID, but when I edged into the doorway the conversation had turned to other matters—war in the news, a friend's tragic abortion.

Alycia had gone AWOL to the nearest town, hitching a ride from a yardman. The town was a gas station, a drugstore that was rarely open, and a dive bar, but she had a boyfriend there. Some decades older than she was.

We covered for her as well as we could. "Alycia's in the shower," announced Jen at the table, the night she left.

We checked the parents' expressions, but no cigar. Poker faces.

David, the next night: "Alycia's in her bunk with cramps." Sukey, the third: "Sorry, Alycia's not coming down. She's in a pretty bad mood."

"That girl needs to *eat* more," said one woman, spearing a roasted potato. Was *she* the actual mother?

"She's thin as a rail," said a second.

"She doesn't do that puking thing, does she?" asked a father. "With the vomit?"

Both women shook their heads. Puzzle unsolved.

"Maybe Alycia has two mothers," said David afterward.

"Two mothers, possibly," said Val, a tomboy who didn't say much. Mostly she parroted.

Val was so small and slight it was impossible to tell her age. Unlike the rest of us, she was from somewhere in the country. She mostly liked to climb. High and nimbly— buildings or trees, it didn't matter. Anything vertical.

"Kid's like a goddamn monkey," a father once said, watching her scale the willow.

A group of parents were drinking on the porch.

"A gibbon," said another. "Or Barbary macaque."

"White-headed capuchin," offered a third guy.

"A pygmy marmoset."

"Juvenile black snub-nosed."

A mother got fed up. "A shut-your-face," she said.

WE WERE STRICT with the parents: punitive measures were taken. Thievery, mockery, contamination of food and drink.

They didn't notice. And we believed the punishments fit the crimes.

Although the worst of those crimes was hard to pin down and therefore hard to punish correctly—the very quality of their being. The essence of their personalities.

IN SOME ARENAS we had profound respect. We respected the house, for instance: a grand old fortress, our castle and our keep. Not its furnishings, though. Several of those we opted to destroy.

Whoever had the most merits, at the end of each week, got to choose the next target. What object would it be? Choice Number One: a china statuette of a rosy-cheeked boy in knee breeches, holding a basket of apples and smiling.

Choice Two: a pink-and-green sampler embroidered with a dandelion and, in a swirly script, the words *Take a Breath Gently. Blow. Spread Your Dreams and Let Them Grow.*

Choice Three: a plump duck decoy with a puffed-out chest and creepy blank eyes, sporting a weird painted-on tuxedo.

"It's a fat faggot duck," said Juice. "A *bowtie* duck. A faggot, like, crooner duck. A Frank Sinatra duck faggot."

He giggled like a maniac.

Rafe, who was out and proud, told him to shut his trap, homophobe idiot.

The winner was Terry that week, and he chose the apple boy. He fetched a ball-peen hammer from the toolshed and smashed in its head.

The house itself, though, we'd never have harmed. Rafe enjoyed setting fires, but limited his arson to the green-house: a pile of hockey sticks and croquet mallets. He also burned stuff in a clearing in the woods—immolated a garden gnome. Its melting plastic gave off thick smoke and a disgusting smell. One of the parents noticed the smoke rising above a stand of pines and elected to stay on the porch, nursing a dry martini.

The smoke dispersed, after a while.

We respected the lake and stream and most of all the ocean. The clouds and the earth, from whose hidden burrows and sharp grass a swarm of wasps might rise, an infestation of stinging ants, or suddenly blueberries.

We respected the treehouses, an elaborate network of well-built structures high up in the forest canopy. They had solid roofs, and ladders and bridges were strung between them to make a village in the sky.

Crude drawings, names, and initials had been etched into their planking by previous vacationers. Those old initials could harsh my mellow fast. Maybe the offspring of the robber barons themselves had carved them—the scions of the emperors of timber or steel or rail, long since turned into baggy triple-chinned matrons of the Upper East Side.

I'd sit up high on a platform, now and then, with others sitting around me, swinging their legs, drinking from soda cans or beer bottles. Idly throwing pebbles at chipmunks. (The little boys put a stop to that, citing animal cruelty.) Braiding each other's hair, writing on each other's jeans, painting their fingernails. Trying to sniff glue from the so-called rec room we didn't use. It never gave you a high.

I'd stare at the initials and feel alone. Even in the crowd. The future flew past in a flash of grim. The clock was ticking, and I didn't like that clock.

Yes, it was known that we couldn't stay young. But it was hard to believe, somehow. Say what you like about us, our legs and arms were strong and streamlined. I realize that now. Our stomachs were taut and unwrinkled, our foreheads similar. When we ran, if we chose to, we ran like flashes of silk. We had the vigor of those freshly born.

Relatively speaking.

And no, we wouldn't be like this forever. We knew it, on a rational level. But the idea that those garbage-like figures that tottered around the great house were a vision of what lay in store—hell no.

Had they had goals once? A simple sense of self-respect? They shamed us. They were a cautionary tale.

THE PARENTS HAD been close in college but hadn't gotten together as a group since then. Until they picked this season for their offensively long reunion. One had been heard to say:

"Our last hur*rah*." It sounded like bad acting in a stupid play. Another one non-joked, "After this, we'll see each other next at someone's funeral."

None of them cracked a smile.

Anonymous, we put descriptions of their careers in a hat. It was a collapsible top hat from the toy closet, where many antique artifacts were kept. (We'd found the klaxon there, and BB guns and a worn-out Monopoly.) We wrote the job titles in block letters so that the handwriting couldn't be easily distinguished, then pulled the papers from the hat and read them out.

A few were professors, with three-month summer vacations. Others went back and forth between their offices and the house. One was a therapist, one a vagina doctor. (A raucous laugh from Juicy, then a quick kick by Sukey to his knee. "You got a problem with vaginas? Say it: vagina. *Va-gi-na*.") One worked as an architect, another as a movie director. (The slip of paper read MAKING GAY MOVIES. "Demerit for homophobia," said Rafe. "When I find out? Major demerit to the closeted queen who wrote *that*. Followed by a beating. It better not be you, Juicy.")

Went without saying: our parents were artsy and educated types, but they weren't impoverished, or they couldn't have afforded the buy-in. A great house didn't rent for cheap. Not for a whole summer. We figured there were probably a couple of charity cases, or at least a sliding scale. David, a techie who dearly missed his advanced computer setup back home, had let slip that his parents rented. Received a demerit for that. Not for the lack of home ownership—we hated money snobs—but for getting soft and confessional over a purloined bottle of Jäger.

Drink their liquor? Sure, yes, and by all means. Act like *they* acted when they drank it? Receive a demerit.

For it was under the influence, when parents got sloppy, that they shed their protective shells. Without which they were slugs. They left a trail of slime.

My own parents were: mother scholar, father artist. My mother taught feminist theory and my father sculpted enormous busty women, lips, breasts, and private parts garishly painted. Often with scenes of war-torn or famine-struck locations. The labia might be Mogadishu.

He was quite successful.

OUR YOUNGER SIBLINGS were a liability in the parent game, constantly threatening to reveal our origins. These belonged to Jen, David, and me.

Jen's eleven-year-old brother was a gentle, deaf kid named Shel who wanted to be a veterinarian when he grew up. He suffered a bout of food poisoning just one week in and had to be tended by their parents, so that ID was made. The mother had adult braces and droopy shoulders, the father a greasy ponytail. He picked his nose while talking. He talked and picked, picked and talked.

We'd thought you grew out of public nose-picking in grade school, but in his case we were wrong. It was actually mind-boggling.

We felt bad for Jen.

And David was toast too. His sisters, IVF twins named Kay and Amy, were straight-up brats and had no interest in the game. They'd sold him out on day two, grabbing and caressing their mother—even going so far as to sit cuddled in her lap, nuzzling her neck. Whispering sweet nothings.

My own small brother, Jack, was a prince among boys. When he contracted poison ivy he came only to me, refusing to ask a parent for assistance. I felt proud. Jack had a sense of duty.

I ran baths for him and sat beside his bunk holding cold compresses to his legs. I smoothed on pink lotion and read to him from his favorite books. He barely complained, saying just, "It does itch, though, Evie."

Jack was hands down my favorite person. Always had been.

Still, he was just a little guy—I worried he might slip up. Vigilance was required.

And at a certain point we made a collective decision: we had to tell the parents about the game. It was getting too hard to evade them through tactical maneuvers alone.

Of course, we'd put a positive spin on the thing. We didn't need to reveal why we'd been playing in the first place. It didn't have to be spoken aloud that our association with them diminished us and compromised our personal integrity. It didn't need to be mentioned that direct evidence of our connection had been known to make us feel physically ill.

We needed a project, we'd just say. Hadn't they deprived us, for the whole summer, of our most dearly beloved playthings and lifelines? Hadn't they confiscated our cell phones, our tablets, all of our screens and digital access to the outside?

We were being held in an analog prison, said David.

THE AUTHORITIES WERE most receptive in the magic hour before dinner, when they were lightly, pleasantly buzzed. Earlier, they tended to be cranky and might refuse. Later, they might be shit-faced and not remember the next morning.

Drinking and talking time, they called it.

It was then that we broached the subject.

"We're playing this game," said Sukey.

"A social experiment, if you will," said Terry.

Some parents smiled indulgently when we explained, while others resisted, trying to master their annoyance. But finally they said OK. They made no promises, but they'd attempt to avoid incriminating us.

Also, we planned to camp on the beach for a few nights, said Rafe.

Practicing self-sufficiency, added Terry.

"Well, now, that's *another* ball of wax," said a father.

One of the professors. His specialty was witch-burning.

"*All* of you?" asked a mother.

The youngest ones nodded—except for Kay and Amy the IVF twins, who shook their heads.

"Good riddance," muttered David.

"But we didn't bring *tents!*" said a second mother.

That mother was low in the hierarchy. Wore long, flowing dresses, in floral and paisley patterns. Once, drunk-dancing, she'd fallen into a potted plant. Bloodied her nose.

I sensed some condescension coming toward her from the other parents. If they were being hunted, she'd be the first one abandoned by the herd. Sacrificed to a marauding lioness whose powerful jaws would rip and tear. Next vultures would peck indifferently at the leftovers.

It would be sad, probably.

Still, no one wanted that mother. We pitied the fool who would be implicated, down the road.

"We'll handle it," said Terry.

"Handle it how?" asked a third mother. "Amazon Prime?"

"We'll *handle* it," repeated Terry. "There are tarps in the toolshed. We'll be fine."

JEN, IMPRESSED BY Terry's masterful attitude, consented to hook up with him in the greenhouse that evening (we'd piled a nest of blankets in a corner). Jen was strong but had notoriously low standards, make-out-wise.

Not to be outdone, the other two girls and I agreed to play Spin the Bottle with David and Low. Extreme version, oral potentially included. Juicy was fourteen, too immature for us and too much of a slob, and Rafe wasn't bi.

Shame, said Sukey. Rafe is hella good-looking.

Then Dee said she wouldn't play, so it was down to Sukey and me. Dee was afraid of Spin the Bottle, due to being—Sukey alleged—a quiet little mouse and most likely even a mouth virgin.

Timid and shy, Dee was also passive-aggressive, neurotic, a germaphobe, and borderline paranoid.

According to Sukey.

"Suck it up, mousy," said Sukey. "It's a *teachable moment*."

"Why teachable?" asked Dee.

Because, said Sukey, she, yours truly, was a master of the one-minute handjob. Dee could pick up some tips.

The guys sat straighter when Sukey said that. Their interest became focused and laser-like.

But Dee said no, *she* wasn't that *type*.

Plus, after this she needed a shower.

Val also declined to participate. She left to go climbing in the dark.

This was while the parents were playing Texas Hold 'Em and squabbling over alleged card counting—someone's father had been kicked out of a casino in Las Vegas.

The younger kids were fast asleep.

Spin the Bottle was a weak choice, admittedly, but our options were severely limited. All the phones were locked in a safe in the library. And we hadn't cracked the combination.

I was apprehensive, but since Dee had pulled out I had

to hang tough. And as it turned out, I got lucky. I only had to French-kiss Low.

Still, unpleasant. His tongue tasted like old banana.

WE SET OUT the next afternoon. Packing and loading the rowboats had taken hours.

"Lifejackets!" screeched Jen's mother from the lawn. She held a wine bottle by the neck, a glass in the other hand, and wore a white bikini with red polka dots. The bottom exposed her ass crack and the top was pretty funny: her nipples showed through the white of the bra cups like dark eyes.

"Make it stop," said Jen, wincing.

"Put on the *lifejackets!*"

"Yeah, yeah. Christ on a *cross*," said Sukey.

We didn't bother with the lifejackets, generally. Except for the little boys. But we were under scrutiny, so I brought a pile of them—bright orange and spotted black with mildew—from the boathouse. They scratched our skin and were bulky. Once we were out of sight, they would come off. Most certainly.

When we pushed away from the moorings various parents waved from the porch and others clustered on the dock. We rushed, worried that they'd betray us with last-minute asinine chitchat. Sure enough, one dimwit yelled: "Did you remember your inhaler?" (Two of us were asthmatics.)

"Shut up! Shut up!" we implored, hands over ears.

None of us wanted to see a man go down that way.

"And what about the EpiPens?" shouted the low-status mother.

I'd been reading a book about medieval society I'd found in the great house library. It had a dusty paper smell I liked. There were peasants in the book: serfs, I guess. Using the filter of that history, and with reference to her flowing-dress wardrobe, I'd come to see her as the peasantry.

We ignored them and rowed with all our strength. Damage control.

"Damn they are *imbeciles*," cursed Low.

I was looking at him with my head cocked, I think—musing. Remembering the taste of banana.

"Mine were cool as a cucumber," boasted Terry.

"Mine didn't give a flying fuck," bragged Juice.

The parents were still trying to communicate with us as our boats drew farther offshore. A few made exaggerated gestures, flapping ungainly arms. Jen's father was doing some sign language, but Shel turned away from his waggling fingers. The peasant mom dove off the dock—in hot pursuit? Taking a dip? We didn't care.

We reached the creek and shipped our oars. Coasting along to the ocean. This was a narrow waterway, and often our vessels would bump the banks, lodge in the muddy shallows and need to be freed.

The water carried us: we were carried.

We lifted our faces to the warmth, closed our eyes, let the sunlight fall across our eyelids. We felt a weight lift from our shoulders, the bliss of liberty.

Dragonflies dipped over the surface, brilliant tiny helicopters of green and blue.

"They live ninety-five percent of their lives underwater," said Jack helpfully. He was an insect fan. A fan of all wildlife, in fact. "In nymph form. You know, larvae. Dragonfly nymphs have big huge jaws. They're vicious predators."

"Is that interesting?" asked Jen, cocking her head.

Not mean, just speculative. She hadn't decided.

"One day they come out of the water, turn beautiful and learn to fly," said Jack.

"Then they drop dead," said Rafe.

"The opposite of humans," said David. "We turn ugly before we drop dead. *Decades* before."

Yes. It was known.

The injustice floated over us with the dragonflies.

"We have been granted much," announced Terry from the prow.

He tried to stand up, but Rafe said he'd flip the boat. So instead he sat down again and made his voice hollow and self-important like a preacher's.

He pushed his glasses up on his nose with a middle finger.

"Yes, we have been given many gifts," he projected. "We, the descendants of the ape people. Opposable thumbs. Complex language. At least a semblance of intelligence."

But nothing was free, he went on. Watching the parents in the privacy of their bedrooms of a night, he'd been struck by the severity of their afflictions. They had fat stomachs and pendulous breasts. They had double asses—asses that stuck out, then sagged and bulged again. Protruding veins. Back fat like stacks of donuts. Red noses cratered by pores, black hair escaping from nostrils.

We were punished by middle age, then long decrepitude, said Terry mournfully. Our species—our *demographic* in the species, he amended—hung out way past its expiration date. It turned into litter, a scourge, a blight, a scab. An atrophied limb. *That* was our future role.

But we should shake it off, he added, suddenly trying to wrap up his speech with an inspiring takeaway. We should summon our courage! Our strength! Like Icarus, we should rise on feathered, shimmering wings and fly up, up, up toward the sun.

For a moment we considered this.

It sounded OK, but was devoid of content.

"You know it was his own fault the wings melted, right?" said David. "His father was a genius engineer. He *told* him not to fly too high or low. Too hot up high, too wet down low. Those wings were *baller*, man. Icarus totally ignored the specs. Basically, the kid was a dick."

2

A SHOCK WHEN we reached the delta, with its braid-ing and shifting sandbars: unwelcome colonists had beached upon our shores.

Before, when we'd come down to the ocean, the dunes had been deserted except for birds and waving grasses. The waterfront had been ours to wander in peace, with its hermit crabs and driftwood and seaweed.

Now there were others. A barbecue. Meat was grilling, and the smell of it carried. There were beach parasols in bright red-and-white stripes.

Where had they come from? You could only get here by boat . . . yep: there it was. A majestic yacht in cream and gold was bobbing loftily offshore.

Up the beach, teens played volleyball.

We felt aggrieved but had no strategy. And no moral high ground, either. It was a public place.

The situation rankled.

If we were patient, though, the sun would soon go down and we'd be on our own. Meanwhile we set up our makeshift shelter on the other side of the braided waters—a pavilion with no walls and the threadbare tarps from the toolshed for a roof, their vinyl peeling off in ragged patches.

We tied the tarps to shrubs on the edge of the dunes, balanced them on fishing rods and ski poles. They wouldn't bear much of a breeze. We had sleeping bags and folded-up clothes for pillows. But at least till dawn came, as the colonists dozed in their luxury berths, we'd have our private empire of salt water and sand.

We watched, munching on soggy sandwiches, as the barbecue-eaters folded their striped umbrellas. From the yacht, a purring and glossy powerboat came up into the shallows.

But hey! What was this?

Sailor types in white uniforms leapt out of the boat carrying bundles. In no time there were sleek-looking tents erected—high-end tents in pearly cream that matched the yacht, alpine-gear logos on the sides. Door flaps and rain flies. Four of them, neatly lined up. A small city above the high-tide mark.

We stared at those handsome tents.

The yacht kids hugged their parents goodnight, as we shuddered. The boat sputtered away. A small fire was built, around which they sat on matching camp chairs. Even their marshmallow sticks were manufactured—we saw them holding the metal skewers over their fire, roasting.

Fine, then. We'd have a fire also. A large bonfire. Our fire would dwarf their fire. It would be magnificent.

We'd brought logs from the woodpile and ancient copies of the *New York Observer* we'd found for kindling. Thanks to Rafe, a can of gasoline. (Marshmallows were for babies, right? Also, we didn't have any.) Juicy had won the latest contest and brought an item to destroy, so we stacked up a glorious pile. I set his chosen object on the top of it: an antique wooden pig in a baby bonnet. With very long lashes.

Before long the flames were leaping high. Black smoke and acrid fumes, including gas and possibly lead paint, sailed downwind toward the yacht kids. It served them right, said Rafe. We cackled like witches over the blaze.

After a while headlamps came bobbing toward us. Yacht kids were wading manfully across the delta, barefoot and tanned, their shorts exactly the right length. Some of us stood up proudly. Others adopted more submissive postures.

"Hey, guys!" said the tall one in the lead. A sweep of blond hair fell over his brow. He wore a polo shirt. He was a billboard for Abercrombie & Fitch. "Dudes! What an awesome burn! I've got some weed. Anyone want a smoke?"

Grinning broadly.

"Shit yeah," said Juice.

And so the empire crumbled.

AT THAT TIME in my personal life, I was coming to grips with the end of the world. The familiar world, anyway. Many of us were.

Scientists said it was ending now, philosophers said it had always been ending.

Historians said there'd been dark ages before. It all came out in the wash, because eventually, if you were patient, enlightenment arrived and then a wide array of Apple devices.

Politicians claimed everything would be fine. Adjustments were being made. Much as our human ingenuity had got us into this fine mess, so would it neatly get us out. Maybe more cars would switch to electric.

That was how we could tell it was serious. Because they were obviously lying.

We knew who was responsible, of course: it had been a done deal before we were born.

I wasn't sure how to break it to Jack. He was a sensitive little guy, sweet-natured. Brimming with hope and fear. He often had nightmares, and I would comfort him when he woke up from them—dreams of hurt bunnies or friends being mean. He woke up whimpering "Bunny Bunny!" Or "Donny! Sam!"

The end of the world, I didn't think he'd take it so well. But it was a Santa Claus situation. One day he'd find out the truth. And if it didn't come from me, I'd end up looking like a politician.

The parents insisted on denial as a tactic. Not science denial exactly—they were liberals. It was more a denial of reality. A few had sent us to survival camps, where the fortunate learned to tie knots. Troubleshoot engines, even sterilize stagnant water without chemical filters.

But most of them had a simple attitude: business as usual.

Mine hid the truth from Jack. And he was already suspicious, because in second grade a teacher had leaked damning info about polar bears, sea ice melting. The sixth mass extinction. Jack also worried about penguins. He was a penguin fanatic—knew all the species and could rhyme them off in alphabetical order and draw them.

We needed to have a sit-down, him and me. But when?

I kept putting it off. The guy was only nine. He still couldn't tell time on a clock that had hands.

Then came the yacht kids, with their medical marijuana and toned physiques. They all went to the same boarding school. And hailed from Southern California, Bel Air and Palos Verdes and the Palisades.

We soon saw it was different there.

"Your folks," said the alpha male, stoned. They'd carried over their camp chairs: no sitting on towels for them. "They got a compound yet?"

"A compound?" asked Sukey, and took a drag. Held it in. She was sitting a bit too close to him, seemed to be basking in the Abercrombie aura. "You mean like—a pot-growing compound?"

"You're funny," said the alpha, and nudged her with a muscular shoulder. Playful.

His name was James. He didn't go by Jim.

"Hilarious," said Sukey, passing the joint to Juice.

"You know, a survival home for chaos time? Ours is in Washington," said another yacht kid. He had a flouncy bandanna tied around his neck.

A really bad idea. Fashion-wise, he seemed to be their equivalent of Low.

"State, not district. Obviously," he added.

"Ours is in Oregon," said James. "Huge solar array. Looks like fucking Ivanpah. *Eleven* backup generators."

Juice had no idea what they were talking about, but that had never stopped him.

"No, yeah. Eleven seems like overkill," he said.

James cocked his head, patient but wise.

"With engineering on compounds, redundancy is key," he explained. "It's about multiple points of failure. Integrated system design."

"No offense," I said, "but we don't have a clue what you're talking about."

"Speak for yourself," objected Sukey.

"Oh yeah?" I said. "OK, Sukey. Educate me."

"Hey, Jack!" she called. "You want dessert? Come over here! These guys brought s'mores!"

Classic deflection. I had to hand it to her.

"I have to go to the bathroom," said Jack, a bit plaintive.

"Just pee in the ocean, little man," said James. "The

ocean's large. It may not be able to beat that plummeting pH, but your piss it can handle."

Jack shook his head, shy.

He'd read a book about scary animals. When you peed in open water, a spiny fish might crawl up the stream of pee and burrow into your penis. A river fish in the Amazon, and possibly mythic, but he'd read the book when he was eight and I suspected he might be recalling it.

"I'll take him," I said, and rose to be a big sister.

"It's number *two*," whispered Jack urgently, as we headed up into the dunes.

"Hold on," I said. "I'll get the toilet paper."

Back in the pavilion, pawing through our supplies by the small light of a lantern, I overheard some talk around the bonfire.

"I heard Missy T.'s compound is in Germany," one yacht kid said to another. "That big bunker under a mountain? A Cold War deal built by the Soviets?"

"Vivos. It's got its own train station."

"Hardened against a close-range nuclear blast."

"The nuclear threat. So quaint."

"It's like, if only. Right?"

"The climate deal makes nukes look kind of sweet. Like being scared of cannons."

"Slingshots."

"A Hyksos recurve bow."

"Canaanite sickle-swords."

I wasn't up on my Canaanites. Maybe I'd google later.

"They've got a DNA vault. Does yours have a vault?"

"Nah. But it does have a seed bank. Non-hybrid."

"Missy. Man. We'll never see *her* ass again. Planes won't be flying, by that time. Even her daddy's Falcon 900."

"Bye-bye, air-traffic control. Bye-bye, Missy."

"Too bad. Man. Missy gives excellent head."

"You got that right. Shee-*yit*."

I had to keep these guys away from Jack.

BUT IT WAS only at nighttime, relaxed by a strain called the Oracle—which retailed at eight hundred bucks an ounce, James said—that the yacht kids discussed their families' preparations for the end-times.

By day they played beach volleyball. For hours. They never seemed to get tired of it, and they had genuine talent. I could picture the girls performing in the Summer Olympics, their shining bodies camera bait. Sometimes they took breaks to fool around in the dunes or lie out—I'd thought that practice vanished back in the twentieth, but the yacht kids didn't care about skin cancer. If they lived long enough to get a bunch of melanomas, they figured, they'd bust out the champagne.

There were two girls and four boys. Their numbers were smaller than ours, but they made up for it in raw personal strength. All of us put together as one team couldn't beat them. Couldn't touch them, even.

We made a joke out of it. Our only face-saving option.

At regular intervals they checked in with their parents, fawning. I heard the kid with the neck bandanna compliment his mother on a nasty purple-and-orange sarong.

The parents were their insurance policy, James said. Diplomatic relations had to be maintained.

"But I mean, even if you acted like jerks, they wouldn't, like, *abandon* you," said Jen, on night two.

The yacht parents had appeared in the late morning, sat drinking in a state of soft paralysis—not unlike our own parents'—until the sun went down, then left again to have a nightcap on the deck. A three-person galley staff had served them lunch and dinner on the beach, plus mixed drinks from a portable bar.

The yacht, I'd noticed on a walk down the beach, bore the gold-lettered name *Cobra*. She wasn't rented, like the great house, but owned outright by James's father—a "VC," as he put it.

That stood for *venture capitalist*, Terry annoyingly informed us as though we didn't know.

I mean, I *didn't* know, technically, but it did ring a bell.

James's mother was missing in action. Probably she was alive, but eyes glazed over when you asked. The father had a third trophy wife, four years older than James. She was a model, said a yacht girl named Tess.

I'd packed Jack off to bed, where he lay next to Shel, reading with his headlamp on at the far end of the pavilion. *Frog and Toad Are Friends*, his favorite book. His second favorite series was *George and Martha*. A pair of kindly hippos. Platonically devoted to each other.

He could read much more advanced books—books without any pictures at all—and liked those too. But he was nostalgic for his old standbys.

"You'd still be their *kids*," pressed Jen. "What, they're going to leave you outside the walls to drown when the flood-waters come up?"

"It's about interpersonal capital," said James. "We prefer not to squander it. What you want is straight A's. You want a perfect record. Unblemished. You want to maintain a 4.0."

Sukey was sitting on one side of him, Jen on the other. I sat across from all three of them, neutral as Switzerland. Personally, I felt no urge to hook up with James. He was handsome enough, or whatever, but he reminded me of margarine. Sneakers that were still stiff from the store. Maybe a roll of thick, bleached paper towels.

"But how do you pull it off?" asked Sukey. "I mean. The drugs. The sex. Just for starters. You get stoned. You get laid. Does that get you a 4.0, in Southern California?"

"Well. Those are coping strategies," said James.

He always had an answer.

"Discretion is the better part of valor," added Tess. "May I have the bong?"

"*Henry IV, Part 1*," said James, passing it over. "Act 5, Scene 4. Falstaff."

"A common misquote," said the neckerchief guy. "Sorry, Tess. 'The better part of valor is discretion, in the which better part I have saved my life.' Lines 3085–3086."

"Falstaff plays dead on the battlefield," nodded James. "Then defends his cowardice."

The yacht kids had their own game. It was called Memorize Shakespeare.

"Demerit, demerit, demerit," said Rafe grumpily.

By LUNCHTIME ON day three we had a food shortage. Someone had left the largest cooler open and gulls perched on the edges, ripping at bread bags with their powerful beaks. Fragments of fruit and cheese littered the sand, and soon even those had been snatched—the gulls were nothing like deer. They didn't scatter when we yelled, or if they did, it was mostly for show. They came right back.

They got up in our grills, pecking. Gobbling.

So we gave up.

I felt bitter about a packet of cookies I'd been saving.

"We need to make a supply run," said Terry, when the finger-pointing ended. "Two of us have to go upriver."

"Or we could go back now," suggested Rafe. "I miss flush toilets."

"No way," said Jen. "I'm not done with James."

Terry shot her a wounded look. She ignored it.

"Let's draw straws," said David.

We used dune grass. We didn't pull it out—Jack warned

us not to hurt the plants—but snipped it neatly with a pen-knife. The shortest blades went to Terry and Rafe, who carried the empty coolers into a boat and began to row. Terry was visibly sulking.

Once the boat disappeared up the creek, a few of us strolled over to where the yacht kids were feasting on lobster rolls. Dee'd found some hand sanitizer near the chef's table and was rubbing it on her body like sunscreen—her own supply must have run out. Sukey and Jen and I picked cans of soda from the yacht kids' cooler, then sat beside Tess under the shade of her umbrella as Low loomed over us, potentially ogling. No room left on her beach blanket.

"It's our last night," she said, dipping a shrimp appetizer in red sauce. "We head to Newport in the morning."

"So soon?" said Sukey.

"Really?" asked Jen.

They both sounded disappointed.

"Supposed to leave yesterday," said Tess, chewing. "But James talked them into staying. For some reason."

Sukey and Jen looked at each other. Sukey took a swig from her can, extended one of her long legs, pointed the toes, turned the foot this way and that. Jen grabbed a shrimp from Tess's cup and popped it in her mouth.

I stared at the shrimps' little black eyeballs on their stalks.

"Watch. They'll be fighting over who gets to hook up with that Aryan douchebag," said Low, as he and I walked away.

When push came to shove, the yacht kids were just too WASP for him. He was a jewel of Kazakh youth, he liked to say—studied history so he could boast about Mongolian hordes. He'd mailed a cheek swab to some genetic-testing service, and the results suggested he was Genghis Khan's nephew.

Some generations removed. But basically, yeah, he said.

Jack and I went down the beach so he could look for periwinkles (rough, northern yellow, and European, he informed me). He was a bit afraid of the waves, so he didn't wade in the surf the way I did. Instead he sat by a tide pool for hours, searching for fish and other small creatures. He carefully replaced each rock he moved, worried that he might hurt a crab.

Me, I sat and gazed at the breakers and sky. That was my preferred activity at the seaside. I tried to disappear into the stretches of water and air. I pushed my attention higher and higher, through the atmosphere, till I could almost imagine I saw the earth. As the astronauts had when they went to the moon.

If you could be nothing, you could also be everything. Once my molecules had dispersed, I would be here forever. Free.

Part of the timeless. The sky and the ocean would also be me.

Molecules never die, I thought.

Hadn't they told us that in chemistry? Hadn't they said a molecule of Julius Caesar's dying breath was, statistically speaking, in every breath we took? Same with Lincoln. Or our grandparents.

Molecules exchanging and mingling, on and on. Particles that had once been others and now moved through us.

"Evie!" said Jack. "Look! I found a sand dollar!"

That was the sad thing about my molecules: they wouldn't remember him.

WHEN WE GOT back the galley staff had switched from lunch to dinner. The sky was banded with faint stripes of pink, and two yacht parents were swimming—a rare event. I saw our green rowboat slip out of the tangle of reeds and brush that marked the mouth of the creek, move into the delta.

There were three passengers now, not two.

"Who's *that*?" asked Jack, squinting toward the boat. I couldn't tell.

Most of our group was over with the yacht kids, where there were food and drinks to be foraged. Only Low and Val hung around our pavilion. As we padded across the sand toward them, our wet shoes hanging from our bent fingers, I saw something looming—something elaborate and dark.

They'd built a massive sandcastle, a tower that rose to a point at the top. It had a circular base and row after row of shelf-like layers ascending in a spiral. They stood on either side of it, sand in their hair and caked under their fingernails, holding cooking pots and spatulas.

"Came to me in a vision," said Low.

"Vision," said Val.

"Of a tower," said Low.

"I can see that," I said.

"It's cool," said Jack, staring up.

"Huh," said Low, as he turned to look at the boat. "Wait. Is that *Alycia*?"

We barely recalled what she looked like.

We waved and waited as the boat drew near. Rafe handled the oars as Terry jumped out and dragged the bow up onto the sandbank, and Alycia, wearing a long silken dress and silver pumps, stepped delicately onto the sand.

The ocean breeze blew her flimsy gown against her body. Hip bones jutted out on either side of her concave stomach.

I'd once seen a picture of sacred cows on the Ganges. Starving.

"What's with the outfit?" I asked.

"No time to change," she said. "Had to make a quick getaway." She kicked the pumps off, pulled the dress over her head. There she stood in a lacy bra and butt-floss thong.

Some yacht dads gazed our way.

"*Evie!*" stage-whispered Jack to me. "She's *naked*!"

"Listen, kid," said Alycia. "What was your name again?"

"Jack?" said Jack.

"Right, right. Well, Jack, I can show you naked if you want. But this isn't it. See this piece of fabric? They call it *underwear*."

"But I can see your regina."

"Jack, it's your lucky day."

She turned from us, splashed through the shallows, and dove. Graceful as a dolphin.

The yacht dads rubbernecked. She front-crawled out past the breakers.

"Why is my day lucky?" asked Jack.

I tousled his hair.

"So she was with that older man in the dive bar in town," said Rafe, coming up the sandbank with the smallest cooler. "She was giving him, like, a lap dance. Her dad walked in and *freaked*. Saying stuff about arresting the guy. He wanted to press charges. For rape. Only statutory, obviously."

"Rape," nodded Val. "But only statutory."

"The guy said he thought she was twenty-four. But get this: turns out the *dad* was there on a Tinder date. Which Alycia knew because she saw the chick swiping on her phone before he got there. Alycia's all, Mom wouldn't like *that* much, would she? So let's just *both* keep our mouths shut. Essentially, blackmail."

"Blackmail," said Val. "Essentially."

I didn't appreciate Alycia's attitude toward Jack, but man. She was no shrinking violet.

AN INVITATION CAME down from the yacht: aboard the *Cobra*, for her last evening anchored in our cove, there would be a party. We were invited.

My bet was, it was Alycia's presence that had inspired the invite.

The girls all wanted to attend, except for Val. The boys didn't, at first, except for Rafe, who liked anything expensive.

We had words.

"You guys are fraternizing with the enemy," said Low.

I sympathized, though these days whenever I felt a kinship with Low it was followed by minor but nagging disgust, remembering the banana. Also an irritation that was close to regret, because Low, without banana breath, and if you changed out his wardrobe for one less hideous, could pass for attractive.

It made me think of how thin the border was between attractive and not, and yet—if it was there, you didn't want to cross it.

But he was right: the yacht was teeming with parents, as bad as ours and probably worse.

"What are you so afraid of?" said Sukey. "Are you gutless? Or just spineless?"

A yacht, a model, and a last night with the Oracle. Passing those up was worse than fraternizing with the enemy, said Sukey. It was a form of self-injury.

Jack wasn't much for parties unless they had a bounce house and birthday cake. He wanted to spend some time with his *Frog and Toad Treasury*, but after that, he said, he had to read another book.

"One of the mothers gave it to me," he said. "Like an assignment. She said I needed to read it."

Plus Jen was determined to go to the party, which meant Shel needed watching, too. So I wouldn't be attending.

I was disappointed.

Sailors broke down the creamy high-end tents, packed them into neat small bundles and loaded them and the yacht kids into the powerboat.

"Goodbye," said James to me before he boarded. We shook hands on it. "I fear we will not meet again. From here to eternity."

"OK," I said.

"But what's your Snapchat?"

"I'm not allowed Snapchat."

"Instagram, then."

When the sun was sinking to the horizon the boat came back to ferry us out. I watched from the shore as Alycia stood at the bow in her thin, rippling dress and bare feet, a figurehead. Her black hair flew out behind her as the boat picked up speed.

She wasn't even wearing a lifejacket. The pilot had made the rest of them sit down, awkward and suffocated in their orange vests. But he hadn't uttered a peep to her, it seemed. Maybe intimidated.

The yacht kids had left us their bag of marshmallows. Pastel colors but full-sized, a rare combo. Jack was delighted. He roasted six at a time, his fingers getting so gooey I had to wash them for him in the lapping tidewater when he was done eating. We sat between our fire and the tall tower from Low's vision—me, Jack, Shel, Val, and Low. Low and I drank warm cans of beer.

Across the water we heard the beat of dance music, and

then we saw fireworks. They blossomed in the sky over the yacht, red, blue, and white flowers. Like it was Independence Day.

And it was, we realized. It was the Fourth.

We played our own music from a boombox, but all we had was a CD of Low's: folk songs. True to his tie-dyes and sandals, Low liked sixties music. "And still somehow, it's cloud illusions I recall. I really don't know clouds . . . at all."

The batteries ran down.

After the music ended, someone suggested ghost stories. We told the one about the one-handed murderer stalking the teen couple who were making out in their parked pickup. They heard some scratching sounds but ignored them. And when they got out of the truck, they found a hook-hand hanging from the door handle.

Jack squealed.

Then there was a clever one about pale eyes at the bottom of a little girl's bed. Suspense, suspense, reveal: they were her own big toenails, shining in the moonlight.

Meanwhile, Low was edging closer to me. One of his legs touched one of mine. Acting like it was a regular movement, I shifted mine away.

And decided to speak. Maybe the time had come. Not for Shel, necessarily—he couldn't lip-read in the dark—but for my brother.

"Hey, Jack? I have to tell you a new story now. But a real one. A story of the future, Jack."

Jack gazed at me sleepily.

"Evie. Is it about the polar bears? And penguins?"

"Yes, Jack," I said. "The polar bears and the penguins. And us."

LATER HE WIPED his eyes and squared his thin little shoulders. My Jack was a brave boy.

I SLEPT LATE the next morning because I'd woken up every time Jack tossed or turned, worried I'd given him nightmares. When I got up, the *Cobra* had weighed anchor. As far as I could see, there was the flatness of the ocean.

Around me the partygoers slept on, silent lumps in their sleeping bags. Except for Rafe, sprawled on the sand beside the embers of our fire in what appeared to be a toga.

And Jack, who showed me the book he was reading. A mother had given it to him, he repeated.

"*Which* mother?" I asked.

Because it was called *A Child's Bible: Stories from the Old and New Testaments.*

"It was the lady who . . . she wears the flowery dresses?"

The peasant mother. Who fell onto plants.

"That lady gave you a *Bible*?"

For our parents religious education wasn't a priority. Driving out of the city for the summer—taking a break from

Minecraft on his tablet—Jack had gazed out the car window, pointed at the top of Bethany Baptist Church, and asked my mother what the long plus sign meant.

"It's a bunch of stories with pictures. There are people and animals, but not as nice as George and Martha," he said.

"Well," I said. "I mean. Who is?"

The first story, Jack told me, had a talking snake in it and a lady who really liked fruit. She had my name!

"I don't like how the snake's a bad guy in it, though. That's mean. Did you know snakes smell with their tongues?"

"What's the story about?" I asked.

"It's like, if you have a nice garden to live in, then you should never leave it."

AROUND NOON, WHEN the others were stirring and rising, David yawned for way too long. I could practically see his tonsils. Then he asked: "Hey. Where's Alycia?"

"Um, she stayed on the boat," said Dee. "Sailed with them to Rhode Island."

"What? Oh. Oh, *no*," said David.

"Her dad's going to be seriously ticked off," said Terry. "And by the way, Rafe ID'd him. Slam dunk. They drove up to the house in the vintage Beamer? Then she jumped out and he followed her. He's the one with the weak chin, covered by a goatee."

"Still don't know which mother it is, though," said Low.

"We'll find out soon enough," said Terry.

"They'll be the ones getting divorced," said Rafe.

He'd taken off his toga—underneath he wore swim trunks I recognized as James's—and was flicking the sand off. It was a sheet. "I wonder what the thread count is on this thing."

"I scored three parent IDs last night," said Jen, yawning. "Anyone want to hear 'em?"

"*Three?*" I asked, incredulous.

"I did better than that. I scored *James*," said Sukey.

"Seriously?" said Rafe. He stopped flicking the sheet, shaking his head. "Me too."

They stared at each other.

Juicy laughed loudly.

The toga sheet had come off James's own berth, said Rafe (like it was proof).

Sukey said she and James had done it in the cockpit. Was that what you called it, on a ship?

Then Dee claimed she and James had fooled around in the yacht's rec room, on top of a pool table. Mostly just kissing. He wanted to do more, but she wouldn't let him.

The three of them tested each other's accounts by referring to a birthmark, then went on to further details of James's buff physique.

"Hey! There are little guys around," I said. "Dial it back, sluts."

Inside a fort of blankets, Jack was reading *George and Martha One Fine Day*.

Jen changed the subject, clearly miffed she'd been left out of the James sex club. Especially since—if you believed

Dee, and I wasn't sure I did, for she had been known to lie—even an uptight mouth virgin had made the cut.

Terry looked smug.

"So the game's practically over," said Jen. "And why? Because there are ass-kissers in our midst."

One of us, cozying up to the model, had bragged his father was a director. Just said his name outright. Rhymed off some titles of movies he'd done. All to impress.

It *was* Juicy. We should have known.

"For shame," said Rafe. "Shame, double shame."

Juice hung his head and spat. Kicked at some glowing embers.

Another, trying to get into James's good graces via a conversation about chaos compounds, had claimed an architect for a mother. Which Jen connected with some talk she'd heard from said mother of renovating a penthouse on Fifth Avenue for a Saudi prince. This was Dee.

And then—the worst, because the most surprising—Terry had been heard making graphic remarks to Tess about the location of female G-spots. How did he know so much? Tess had asked, according to Jen. Said Terry: Because he had a gynecologist in his family.

We *all* knew who the doctor was. She'd tried to lecture us collectively, over a not-good dinner of tofu dogs, about the risks of human papillomavirus.

Terry groaned and reached for a beer. "It was the Oracle, man!"

"You're blaming it on weed?" said Sukey. "Pathetic."

I felt deflated.

"You don't win till you're the last kid standing," pointed out Low. "A lot of us still have a chance."

"There's still what, four of you left?" said Jen. "If Evie and Jack count as one?"

"Yeah, *I'm* still in," said Sukey.

"And me," said Rafe.

"And me," said Low.

Still, the wind was out of our sails. The currency of the game had been devalued.

"But listen, guys," said Low, "for reals. Up at the great house, when we got food, they said some weather's on the way."

"What *kind* of weather?" asked Dee, startled. She startled easily.

"What kind of weather *is* there?" said Low. "A big storm. They said if we weren't back by this morning, they'd come down and get us."

We argued about compliance a bit, whether the parents were making up the weather as a pretext for our return—it was hurricane season, sure, but the storms didn't usually get bad till late August or September.

Our resistance was halfhearted, though. In the distance, over the water, we saw a low bank of clouds. A chill wind was blowing, and the surface of the ocean was flat gray.

Grudgingly we packed up, tore down the peeling tarps and ski poles, and bundled it all into our vessels.

Jen, next to me in the rowboat, was still sulking over James. David was preoccupied, jiggling a leg anxiously, and

Jack was melancholy, drawing macaroni penguins in his notebook.

I pushed off and began to row, since the others didn't offer.

Glancing back, I saw no obvious signs of our stay except some pockmarks and footsteps, charred wood and ashes. A few sticks out of place, maybe. And the tall tower, collapsing as the tide came in. We knew the drill: leave no trace.

Of course, there would always be traces. The trick was to hide them.

We'd left some molecules behind for sure, I thought as I pulled and pushed. But nothing that said who we were. Just skin and nails and hair, cast far and wide into the sea.

3

WE WERE TIRED and dirty, rowing upriver. Everyone wanted showers, and the partyers wanted hangover cures. I was yearning for a few minutes alone.

So when the great house hove into view across the lake I felt like it was home. I could imagine my whole life had been lived there, instead of a drab building in Greenpoint.

I saw myself swimming in the lake every summer, lying on my back in a grassy field naming the constellations. Running full tilt down the dirt road, where the two rows of trees joined in a long arch overhead, my arms flung wide.

Roaming wild in the tumbling woods.

BUT THE PARENTS were in panic mode.

A few cars were still parked in the crescent drive, but most had been driven inland on a supply run. Some fathers were headed outside to nail plywood onto the windows. They stopped us in the foyer and asked Rafe and Terry to help them with the nailing.

Sexist pigs, muttered Sukey. She followed them outside, demanding a hammer.

Jack and Shel took off into the woods.

In the bathrooms mothers were filling buckets from the tubs. In the kitchen they were sorting and counting batteries, lining up flashlights and headlamps on counters. The coolers we'd taken to the beach were commandeered.

Someone was messing with a radio, and phones were charging in every spare outlet.

There was a prickle in the air.

I helped them scoop ice cubes from the freezers into deli bags. My fingers went numb. A TV on the wall showed swirling formations. Forecasters were talking about categories and wind speeds, paths and cones and bands. We'd heard the terms before. There were mandatory evacuations and stubborn folks "riding it out." Some who would die of sheer stupidity.

Some who would die because they loved their homes. Some who were frail and old. Some others trying to rescue them.

A couple of us took advantage of the newly relaxed rules: carrying an ice bucket for a mother, I passed an open bedroom door. Saw Low fully relaxing on a parental bed. Flipping channels with a remote, trolling for entertainment.

"Shirker!" I said, pointing my finger.

Someone came up beside me. A short father. With a paunch.

He stood there, hands on his hips in a womanish fashion, glaring in.

It was a self-righteous glare. Low took in the situation instantly. His face fell.

"Lorenzo, *get up* off that bed," said the father.

Low complied. Lethargically. Defeated.

"You are *so* busted," I said.

I left him to his humiliation. Saw Jen checking her makeup in a hallway mirror and told her about the Low ID. "One down, three more to go," she said.

In the parlor I caught sight of my mother kneeling in front of a liquor cabinet, as though before an altar. "We could also use bourbon, sherry, vodka, and vermouth," she told her cell. I waved at her, since we hadn't seen each other in days. She saw me but ignored me completely. "Make it at least four Bulleits," she said to the phone. "Wait. Do they have the jumbo size?"

EVENTUALLY I GOT to worrying about Jack, so I went outside looking. Jogged past the tennis courts, heading into the treehouse grove.

No Jack there, but I spotted the twin girls playing tug-of-war with a doll. They didn't hear me approach, I guess, because before I had a chance to call out—planning to ask if they knew where my little brother was—the one named Kay abruptly let go of the doll. Her sister fell onto the ground, flat on her back.

Then Kay picked up a rock, leaned over and bashed her sister on the head with it. Hard.

"What the fuck!" I yelled.

I ran over to Amy—Kay grabbing the doll and scurrying away, grimacing—and fell to my knees in the grass.

"Amy! Amy!"

Blood on the forehead. A visible dent. The kid was pale. No movement.

"Shit, shit, oh shit," I said.

I hadn't been trained for this. My Skills for Survival camp in the Poconos had focused on three-legged races and Capture the Flag.

But she was small and light, so despite a voice in my head that asked, *Should she even be moved? Oh well*, I picked her up and stumbled back to the house carrying her limp body.

DAVID'S MOTHER WENT into hysterics, while someone else called 911. The only doctor among the parents—Terry's mother, as we knew now—was miles away, filling a shopping cart.

Amy might be concussed, someone said. She'd been knocked out. Despite the fact that no one thanked me, I felt mildly heroic.

By the time the ambulance pulled up and a team of paramedics dismounted, the storm prep had been put on hold. David's mother leaned over Amy on a sofa, my own mother leaned over *her*, and some fathers clustered around.

"Is she in a persistent vegetative state?" quavered David's mother. "Does she have *brain damage*?"

My mother patted her shoulder robotically with a flat, board-like hand. "Unlikely," she said. "From a statistical perspective."

A natural nurturer, my mother.

The paramedics came in and did their thing—I wasn't close enough to see, but soon it was clear that Amy would survive, non-comatose. Her legs, clad in red-striped ankle socks and pink Hello Kitty Mary Janes, scissored back and forth on a couch cushion, kicking. I heard a telltale whine. "Mommy! Kay's so *mean*! She *hit* me! She took *Lacy*!"

I still needed to find Jack. Maybe Kay had hit *him* with a rock, too. Run away with *his* most prized possession (a two-foot-tall plush penguin called Pinguino). Maybe the budding psycho was doing some stockpiling of her own: other kids' toys.

A few minutes in, I flicked on a light in the pantry looking for food and saw David, who'd been notably absent from the crowd around his injured sister. He was sitting on the floor in the corner. With a bottle beside him.

"You didn't get enough to drink *last* night?" I said.

"I drank Cokes on the yacht," he said. "Stayed sober. Thought I had to monkey-wrench."

"Say what?"

"I didn't know Alycia'd *stay* there," he said. "She didn't

say anything. Too busy flirting with some pig of a father. It's on her. Right? Sleeping with the enemy. And I didn't know a storm was coming, either. I had no idea."

"What do you mean, monkey-wrench?"

"Those yacht parents are the worst. *Those* are the people that ate the planet."

"David. What did you do?"

"I was thinking of a puncture in the fuel tank first. But you know. Gas in the ocean, killing fish. I didn't want to sink to their level. So I just coded a little virus into the nav system," said David.

I stared at him. I'd had no idea he was so hardcore.

"You should have seen those parents. Heard them. They were like rotten meat."

"But. That virus. You mean . . ."

"The yacht won't make it to Newport," he said. And raised the bottle, took a swig.

It was champagne. It foamed around his mouth. Dripped down his neck and soaked his shirt.

"Listen," I said. "They motored off with no problem. Their crew can fix it. Probably have already."

David shook his head. "I don't think so."

He looked so dejected that I sat down beside him, nudged him with my shoulder.

"They're all about backup systems. Right? And they're filthy rich. They'll land on their feet. I'd bet on it."

By and by I heard a noise of hammering, and then a mother asking for help finding dog food.

Storm prep was on again, and I left David to his guilt. I had to find my brother.

IN THE ATTIC Jack had set Pinguino and his book collection on his bottom bunk, but he was nowhere to be seen.

In the greenhouse Jen and Terry were making out. They pulled apart when I stuck my head in.

"Really?" I said.

"Hey, they told us to harvest the produce," said Jen.

"And we couldn't *resist*," said Terry, full of himself. "I mean this is our *place*. We have history here."

"*Our* place? Gross. Please shut up," said Jen.

They went back to picking cherry tomatoes off a vine. The greenhouse was four walls of broken glass and splintered struts, but a few vegetables still grew in its mess of weeds.

In the toolshed there was no one.

In the boathouse there was no one.

In the treehouses there were only initials.

But after a while, in a muddy cove of the lake that was hidden from view of the house by a screen of scrub and bulrushes, I found the small boys.

They had a shoebox and two nets—butterfly nets from the toy closet. They were squatting beside the box, putting the lid on, when I approached.

"Jack, I've been looking for you *everywhere*," I said.

"Sorry, Evie," he said.

"What are you doing down here?"

"We're collecting."

He liked to make nature collections—moss, flowers, rocks—and build miniature dioramas in trays or baking pans. He'd nestle water features among the plants, sometimes containing minnows or tadpoles he'd scoop up in cups and jars and place into his scenes. Pretty soon he'd get concerned for their well-being and carry them back to the lake.

One collection had been so beautiful I wanted to shrink myself and live in it. There were tiny trees made of twigs he'd snapped off, shrubs made of lichen, a bridge of curved bark. There was a cave made of rocks and a chain of ponds in mussel shells. In a shady bower of leaves and sticks hung a silvery chrysalis, out of which he'd hoped a butterfly would emerge.

It did not.

"OK. But you should probably come back to the house."

Shel shook his head and signed something—he'd taught Jack some basic sign language.

Shel could talk, but he almost never did.

"We gotta do more," said Jack. "Evie. It's *important.*"

"The storm's important too."

"It's *for* the storm," he said. Determined.

"Listen. I'll give you one more hour. Deal?"

He looked at Shel, who nodded.

"And don't get separated, either," I said.

"Buddy system," said Jack. "Pinkie swear."

THE CONVOY HAD returned with a fresh load of plywood. Fathers were getting irritable. Fewer tools than hands, so we had to take turns with the hammers.

When Jack got back he came to me and showed me a bleeding finger.

"What happened?" I asked. Then got distracted: Kay was slinking past us, dragging her sister's doll by one leg. The doll had taken a beating. Seemed to be missing the other leg, and its hair had been shorn off. It had a scalp of blond plugs.

"Tell you later," said Jack.

I'd just turned back to window-covering when a hand landed on my shoulder.

Alycia's father, the one with the goatee and Tinder date.

"Uh—Edie, is it?"

"Eve."

Their family clearly had trouble with names.

"Eva. Do you know where my daughter is?"

Damn. Why me?

I'd tell him about the yacht, I decided. But would I tell him about possible difficulties with its navigation?

I didn't want to implicate David.

And yet.

I stood there with the hammer. It felt heavy.

"She didn't choose to come back with us," I said.

His mouth hung slightly open.

"I'm sorry. You mean she's still down there? All by herself? On the beach?"

Beside me, Sukey stopped hammering also.

"She sailed for Newport," said Sukey, blunt as always. "On a yacht called the *Cobra*. Owned by a venture capitalist."

"Ha ha! No seriously," said the goatee father.

"Seriously," said Sukey.

"You've got to be kidding me!"

"Nope," said Sukey, and went back to hammering.

When the father turned away he seemed stunned.

Then the gynecologist mother came down the steps from the breakfast room. "They're saying it's a Cat 4. Winds up to 140!"

"All this hysteria's for nothing," said the short father. (Low's, I recalled with a surge of satisfaction.) He was holding a beer bottle. Hadn't lifted a finger to help cover the windows, just watched and critiqued. "You'll see."

Another mother stuck her head out the door. "Hey. Where's Alycia?"

Not again. I sighed.

"On a yacht headed for Rhode Island," I said.

"They've got excellent food on that boat," piped up Dee. "The chef used to work at Chez Panisse."

I opted not to look at the mother's face right then. Everyone knew Alycia didn't eat.

WE STILL DIDN'T have the windows done when the rain got harder. The fathers gave up, clearing throats, shaking heads, retreating to mix their drinks.

When the dinner whistle blew we merged into the dining room, hungry. Rain was drumming steadily on the roof, but the room was enormous and sound faded there. A splendid chandelier hung from a high beam—it had once been Teddy Roosevelt's. Or so a three-ring binder claimed. It contained the house's history. "The dude in the wheelchair," Juicy had nodded knowingly when we read it.

There was also a long table fit for a king. Still didn't hold us all. The house hadn't been built for this many guests—special permission had been received to house us in the attic—so card tables were set up along one wall to hold the overflow. Normally we raced each other to sit at those card tables at dinner, due to their reduced proximity to parents.

But there was no food now. The king's table was empty except for two slumping bags of ripple chips.

A rumble of discontent.

"Head count!" yelled Jen's mother.

"*Dinner*," said Sukey firmly.

"It's spaghetti," said Jen's mother. "Set the table, then."

David did knives while I did forks. At the cutlery drawer I whispered: "Did you tell anyone else you messed with the yacht's computer?"

He shook his head, downcast. "Do I have to?"

"Let me think on it," I said.

But then Alycia's parents came in. Agitated.

"The Coast Guard got a distress signal!" said her mother. "From the boat she's on!"

"Are they sending a rescue team?" asked Jen's father. "First responders?"

"We don't know! We don't know!" shrieked the mother.

"We don't know," clarified the father.

As I FORKED up pasta, it struck me the parents had put their drinking on hold for at least two hours. The voice of the weatherman had told them to prepare, so they prepared.

They didn't do well with long-term warnings. Even medium-term. But they still had reflexes.

"Um Evie, there might be a little problem," said Jack as I was finishing.

He'd popped up behind me.

I followed him down the steps to the basement. Shel was there, in front of a closed door—a door to the room with the water heater in it, if I remembered right.

"Listen."

I put my ear to the door. First I heard nothing, then a fizzing sound—no, a buzzing.

"See, they came *out* of the hive! We didn't know they would do that."

"You're telling me—"

"We wanted to bring all the bees but we didn't have time. This hive is the biggest."

I stepped back from the door.

"Jack. You brought a *beehive* in?"

"One raindrop can *kill* a bee," he said.

I thought of him and Shel stumbling across the grounds carrying the beehive and almost raised my voice.

When we got upstairs again, only parents were left in the dining room. The wind was rising. I saw it moving a loose piece of plywood and heard the branches of the big willow scraping the glass walls of the breakfast room.

Outside was pitch black, save for the orange spots of the lamps that lit the footpaths.

"Where *is* everyone?" asked Jack.

Where they were was watching TV in the library. The image was simple: the steady, spiral whirling of the storm.

"Can we watch something else?" said Juice.

"Hey, guys, turns out there's a beehive in the house," I said.

THE STORM HIT full-force in the middle of the night.

I'd lain sleepless on my pad on the floor, listening to the shudder of the walls as gusts buffeted them. So I was wide awake when a branch crashed through the attic window and kept on going, tearing part of the roof off as it fell.

The power'd been knocked out: flipping the light switch did nothing. Rain slanted through the gaping hole.

There was a stampede. I fumbled my way to Jack, who sat on his bed holding Pinguino, and a crowd of us surged down the staircase. Parents were milling, and in the babble of voices flashlights got switched on and candles got lit.

"It's the big willow!" someone cried.

In the breakfast room water was pouring onto the table and chunks of plaster fell from the ceiling as rain blew in the smashed floor-to-ceiling window. The trunk of the willow was slanting overhead. By lantern light I saw outside: the ragged mass of its black roots was torn from the ground.

"Someone! Where's the plywood?" yelled a father.

"Get me the cordless drill!" yelled another.

"What's that?" asked Low, pointing out the broken window to the wide lawn beyond.

"Light, please," said a mother, and flashlights pointed.

"It's shiny," said Jack.

"It's *water*," said a father.

"The lake is in the yard," said Jack.

There was water all around.

"What does the Weather Channel say? How many inches have we had?" asked someone else.

Too many people were shouting. Flashlight spots danced frantically over the yard, an expanse of rainwater that seemed to stretch everywhere. Its surface was slashed and pocked by more rain falling, a blur of pinpricks.

Another meeting was convened in the dining room, but I couldn't hear what the parents were saying over the pounding

of the rain and the drilling of the fathers. The unlit chandelier loomed over us, a dim glass jellyfish in the dark reaches
of the ceiling. Candles sputtered on the table. We shifted
from foot to foot. Someone had bad B.O.

Since we couldn't hear the parents we muttered among
ourselves. Sandbags. Could you buy those? Or did you have
to make them?

I already missed the electricity. With no light or power
and some of the walls and ceilings breached, I felt a curious
passivity creep over me. What defenses did we have? What
could we even do?

When the talk trailed off the crowd moved, bodies bus-
tling out of the room again and carrying us along.

"So what's the plan?" I asked the nearest mother. "I
couldn't hear."

"Two hundred garbage bags," she said. "And plenty of
duct tape."

THERE WERE TASKS, there was wet and cold, there was the
black overhead of the sky. I don't remember the events in
order. I know we splashed outside with some fathers to help
with weatherproofing. We couldn't see what they did, but it
didn't look technologically advanced.

I held an umbrella over a father's head and gazed down at
my feet with the headlamp I'd been given: they were planted
in water. The bottom edges of the basement windows were
already a couple of inches submerged.

The house was an island.

During a lull in the wind I heard voices above me and craned my neck to look. Skinny legs in cargo pants dangled off the roof.

"Hey!" I called. The legs disappeared, and a head and arms came into view. Val. Holding a white garbage bag in one hand. It ballooned out in the wind.

"What are you *doing* up there?" I called.

"Roof hole! I'm covering!" yelled Val.

They'd put a kid on the roof in a lightning storm.

WE HUDDLED TOGETHER on mattresses and sleeping pads at the dry end of the attic. Within hours the bags Val had taped over the hole were sagging and gaping: when I woke I saw water had spread farther and farther across the room. There was a tide of wetness on the floor. Cool air was gusting in around the billowing plastic.

Jack wasn't beside me, but Juicy was. Snoring. Low lay in a fetal position in the corner. The sleeping bags were dingy, the pillows were yellowed, and faces were grimy in the gray light of morning. We'd all slept in our dirty clothes.

"Volunteers! Volunteers!" yelled a woman.

The peasant mother was leaning in the door. Her salt-and-pepper hair stuck out in small braids all over her head. Looked like someone had tried for cornrows and ended up with a grimy shag rug.

"We need the boats!" she said. "Any strong swimmers

here? The boats got out of the boathouse! The boats are on the loose!"

Juicy and Val and I put on our wet shoes and thumped down the stairs. In the front yard, which was higher ground than the back, we saw parents in cars, desperately trying to fit them onto a grassy knoll that loomed up on one side of the drive.

We waded across the back lawn, water up to our knees. Beneath the surface the grass had turned to mud, and my feet sank. I was glad to get to the real lake, where at least there was deep enough water to swim in.

We swam.

The water was brown instead of blue. Leaves and sticks made fleets of litter and circled lazily. I saw a yellow beach ball floating, a red rubber slipper, a toddler's plastic dinner plate divided into sections. There was a wading pool, blue and orange and printed with fish. Tangles of purple skipping rope and a basketball hoop.

I thought: Water's going where it isn't allowed. Dryness was a temporary state. Like safety.

I swam through the murky brown, Juicy and Val beside me, flinching every time my feet knocked against a solid object.

The boats had lodged under the side of a dock on the far side of the lake, near a broken-down fishing hut. Val slipped a bungee cord from her pocket—always well equipped— and hooked the two canoes together. Juice and I each took a rowboat.

SOME FATHERS MADE a fire in the library fireplace. The warmth didn't permeate far—a cold draft crept through the house from the breakfast room and the roof—so we hung around the hearth nursing hot drinks. The mothers who usually did the cooking appeared to be on strike. I'd seen two of them snorting lines of coke in the bathroom.

Alycia's mother was sitting in an armchair in the corner of the library without moving—been there a long time. She'd wandered down a distant road. A mental road, said Rafe.

First she'd knitted with total focus, then she'd unraveled the knitting. She was covered in a blanket, and when I went up to her to ask if she needed something—a courtesy I rarely extended to a parent—the dip in the blanket, in her lap, was full of cut-up pieces of yarn.

She acted like I wasn't there, plus she was holding scissors. I figured I'd move on.

"She's dissociating," I heard a mother tell a father. The therapist, probably. "Detachment from reality. It's like that time the four of us went down to Cabo. Remember?"

"Oh right. The time with the tranny sex worker? And the donkey in the sombrero?"

"Bill, *Jesus*," said the mother. "We don't say *tranny* anymore."

The day felt formless, a crazy woman in her chair snipping, some fathers beside the fireplace talking in stoned voices about utopia. (Their pot was garbage next to the Oracle, said Terry with contempt. But he'd filled a freezer bag with it anyway.) Time ran together in the dark. Day for night, night for day, and the lost power made the house static and dim against the wind.

Then I had an idea.

"We should get our phones back," I told Terry.

After all, the bylaws had been suspended. The parents were consulting their own phones, those who weren't cutting up scarves or breathing Purple Kush.

So we waited till the stoned fathers were lying on their backs. They crossed their legs and expressed some thoughts about a workers' paradise. It would have saved us, said one. If anything could, said another. Capitalism had been the nail in the coffin, said a third.

They'd switched their pot out for cigarettes and were trying to blow smoke rings, but the rings had no holes. Looking over my shoulder to make sure we were still being ignored, I tiptoed over to the painting that hid the safe.

I liked that painting. In front of pine trees with snow-tipped boughs, a brown bear stood on his hind legs. His front paws hung in front of him as though he was begging, and behind him stretched a bright-blue lake, with mountains on a far shore. His posture was humble, his head cocked to one side. Inquisitive.

Before, I'd assumed he was a bear of the past. A rustic bear of the 1800s. The robber barons might have shot him and used him for a rug. But now I could see him as a bear of the future, when men had disappeared from the hills and fields, their old paths overgrown. And the bears and wolves were masters again.

Terry helped me lift it off the hook. The safe door was ajar, and inside were all our phones and tablets. Stacked up like pirate's treasure, a snarl of chargers and battery packs behind them.

Better than diamonds and pearls.

I was smiling so hard I didn't even know it for a minute. Then I thought: *I'm smiling.*

"Yes! Yes! Free the people!" crowed Terry.

At that point we didn't care if the stoned fathers noticed.

We dumped some magazines out of a basket and piled in the phones. Then we went striding through the house with our shoulders thrown back, triumphant. We yelled out names and passed out bounty. We showered them with devices. We were heroes and paragons. Liberators and saints.

There *was* still the problem of the power outage, but we agreed to share our spare battery packs.

"Now we can do *everything*!" said Jen.

Juicy unleashed a string of happy obscenities. Val nodded with an air of satisfaction.

Low had tears in his eyes.

I WAS WORRIED about Jack, with all the standing water. He wasn't much of a swimmer. So I made him and Shel wear the moldy lifejackets over their beekeeping suits.

From the wraparound porch I watched them wade across the lawn. They were pulling one of the rescued canoes on a cord, and it was piled high with boxes. A mystery. At the edge of the woods they tied the canoe to a tree, and then struggled to carry their boxes toward the treehouses. I watched as their backs and shoulders receded, small columns of white and orange.

"Has everyone got their phones?" asked Terry. We fussed with our devices, scrolling or typing or plugging drained phones and tablets into battery packs. "The backup batteries? Everyone? I got one left. A Hello Kitty case? With pink sparkles?"

"Amy's," said David.

"The twins have *phones* already? They're, like, *eight!*" said Sukey.

"Eleven," said David. "They're small, and they do a baby act."

"*Ass*hats," said Sukey.

"That Kay's a straight-up psycho," said Jen.

"Word," said David.

WITH THE GRAY daylight dimming, no sign of the storm letting up, and the water still rising, we planned to sleep on the ground floor—lay our pads and bags down wherever we found room.

Jen and David and I went outside to round up the little

boys. Their canoe was still moored at the trees' edge, tied to a branch. We waded through knee-high water until we reached higher ground, shoes heavy with mud.

"Jack! Shel!" we yelled into the trees. "Are you there?"

"Evie, we have to stay," called down my baby brother.

"Up a tree? In a *storm*?" I yelled.

"I'm going up," said Jen. "It's too dark. I can't sign with Shel from down here."

Jack's tree was connected to others by bridges made of planks and ropes. His treehouse was the largest, but the platform was crammed so full of boxes we could barely step onto it. Jen signed rapidly at Shel—she was impatient, shivering in her shorts.

"What are all the boxes, Jack?" I asked.

"You know how, in that book the lady gave me, after they left that beautiful garden they got in a really big flood?"

"He's reading the *Bible*?" said Jen.

"We can talk about your book later," I said. "For now we should go in. It's not safe here, you see."

"Evie," said Jack. "We have to save the animals. Like Noah did."

That was when I looked around at the stacked boxes. I saw two birdcages, fluttering movements inside them. I saw holes punched in one box, two box, three box, four. A furry brown snout poked out of the grille on a plastic pet carrier.

"We collected them," said Jack.

"Wild animals?" I asked.

"A bunny's the one that bit me," he said. "Maybe he thought my finger was a carrot."

"You guys gotta come into the house now," said Jen.

"But we *can't*," said Jack, and Shel grabbed her arm and signed at her frantically.

"Why not, Jack?" I asked. "Aren't you getting cold out here? And hungry?"

"We have some food. And we moved *everyone*. Plus our owl won't go in the house, no way. He's hurt."

"Your *owl*?" I asked.

Jack pointed up into the branches. I couldn't see.

"He's a barn owl. He has a broken wing."

"You realize rabbits and owls don't really chill together, right?" said David. "It's not like picture books where woodland creatures put on dresses and square-dance at picnics."

"But see, we have to *feed* him. He can't *fly*," said Jack.

"The 'rents could notice if these guys aren't in the house tonight," said Jen to me. "It's *me* who'll be punished."

"We're not going," said Jack, and lifted his chin.

Shel shook his head in solidarity. Jen moved toward him—maybe to grab his arm—and he did something, quick, that surprised me.

He pulled a thick metal bracelet out of the pocket of his hoodie and clicked it onto his wrist, a silver glint in the dimness. Then he clicked again.

He'd handcuffed himself to the treehouse.

4

THAT WAS HOW our exile started: Shel and Jack and a pair of handcuffs. Jack said they'd found them in the toy closet, but they weren't toys. Jen and I had to stay with our brothers, and David stayed out of guilt over the shipwreck. He was glad to get away from the unraveling mother.

A miracle, though: our cells had signals. Through the plastic bag hers was in, Jen read aloud to David and me about the floodwater. It was full of oil and sewage. There were bodies in there, human and dog and bird and cow. There were pesticides and fertilizers and drain cleaner and antifreeze.

It was a toxic soup.

I texted my mother our location, in the unlikely event that she was worried about Jack.

She sent back an emoji of a tulip.

"Don't sweat it," said Jen. "It's drinking and talking time."

The three of us accepted crackers from the boys and called up weather apps. Rain. Icons of clouds with bolts of lightning. Icons of hail. A spiral one I hadn't seen.

"That's 'hurricane,'" said David helpfully.

Coastal flood warnings, severe thunderstorm warnings— it seemed like a word salad in a clean red font. Who knew what it meant? Who knew what was coming?

Later we slept hunched together on a nearby platform— smaller than the Ark, but decently covered—sharing some blankets and pillows Jack and Shel had brought. They smelled of cat pee.

In the morning Jack showed me his menagerie. The sharp-nosed animal I'd seen in the pet carrier was a possum that kept itself busy gnawing on the wire door with its sharp yellow teeth. Did serious damage, too. There were two doves, a robin, and a small brown bird in a homemade-looking mesh deal. There was a murky terrarium Jack said held crayfish, toads, and a salamander. There were plastic food containers with holes poked in the top, full of silty water and minnows, and a big, fat fish in a cooking pot. There were brown field mice skittering back and forth in a drawer with a sheet of clear plastic duct-taped on top of it.

"How about the bees?" said David. "Are they still in the flooded basement?"

"Of course not!" said Jack, indignant. "They went back in their hive. So we brought it outside."

"Hey!"

It was Sukey, at the base of the tree. Others. Umbrellas and hooded ponchos and raincoats. Upturned faces. Rafe, Terry, Dee, Low, Juicy.

"We're moving out here!" shouted Sukey.

"You don't *want* to," I called down. "It's cold and wet!"

"Don't care!" yelled Low. "It's *vile* in there!"

THEY STRAPPED UP the tarps from the beach to extend our roof cover. They found a stash of paint-spattered ground-sheets and swarmed over the canopy, lashing the bright-blue vinyl to the treehouse posts. They stretched them between platforms, over nets and ladders.

I felt restless. If they didn't want to go back to the house, whatever, but *I* did. I wanted the fireplace and the cabinets packed with snack cakes and miniature powdered donuts. The indoor plumbing.

I asked Dee, then Terry, then Rafe what the deal was, but they refused to talk about it. It was only when Sukey finished setting up her sleeping bag, weighing it down with rocks, that I got a straight answer: during the night the older generation had dosed itself with Ecstasy.

No one knew if it had been a plan or covert action, but they'd promptly ascended new heights of repulsive.

It was true Juicy and Terry had watched them fool

around from behind slatted doors at the beginning—even Low had done it. Out of a sense of desperate boredom, soon after the phones were taken away. Also vengeance. And scorn.

Now they regretted it. Maybe they'd had had stronger stomachs, back then.

"Plus that was just like, normal old-people sex," said Juicy.

"How would you know?" said Rafe.

"Like, couples," said Juicy. "This is . . . like, everything."

"They're walking around butt naked," said Low.

"I saw two fathers and Dee's mother in a three—" started Juicy.

"Stop!" shrieked Dee. "Stop! Stop! Stop! Stop!"

"Shut up, Juicy," said Rafe. "No names. That's cruel and unusual punishment."

"They're writhing and moaning all over the place," said Sukey. "Biggest shitshow I ever saw."

"Shitshow," said Val, nodding. "Biggest."

The nodding looked strange, since her face was upside down. She was hanging off a rope ladder by her knees.

"They gave up completely on fixing the holes," said Sukey. "The water keeps pouring in and they just smile and chew their bottom lips. And stroke each other's junk."

LATER I FOUND myself sitting on a rock at the edge of the woods, waiting. Terry and David had drawn the short straws and taken the canoe to get food, and a few of us were hanging around at the water's edge to help them unload. I watched them paddle across the yard toward us.

Branches thrashed back and forth in the wind.

"Those trees look just like girls freaking out," said Juicy. He flung his arms randomly around his head, his mouth wide open. "They look hysterical."

"You're *such* a fucking sexist," said Sukey. "When you say shit like that, I kind of feel like degloving your testes."

"Degloving?" asked Juicy. "Huh. What's that?"

They were drowned out by the wind, thankfully, as Sukey explained it to him. I could only hear snatches of dialogue. ". . . peel the skin back . . ."

Leaves flew into my face, leaves and dirt, until I had to hold my arms up in front of me. The sky was flashes and booming thunder.

"Come on! Come on!" shouted Jack behind us.

Terry and David paddled faster, but the canoe was carrying too much and moved at a lazy pace. Water slopped over the sides.

Lightning struck. A direct hit: the weathervane on top of the house. It sent up a fountain of sparks.

Terry shrieked, leaping up in the canoe. He toppled out. The boat capsized.

I saw cracker boxes soaking up water, cans sinking. I saw bags of cheese popcorn spin away in the dark.

So we had to wade into the toxic soup again.

I COULDN'T GET to sleep when the others did. There was no lightning, but the water was pouring down.

I fumbled around on the platform for my headlamp, stepped over Jen and Sukey, and walked across two rope ladders to the Ark.

Jack was fast asleep, his small face lit by a lantern that hung from the single, low roof beam. But the animals in their cages were scratching around. Chirping. Squawking. I figured most of them were probably nocturnal.

I squatted down and lit up the face of the possum. Its snout twitched as it sniffed at me. Then an animal I couldn't identify turned away from my light—a fox? Could Shel have caught a fox?

My mouth tasted bad: no toothpaste around.

Rustling next to my ear. A flurry. Something brushed against my cheek. A sharp claw almost pierced my shoulder.

"What!" I said.

It scrabbled down my arm and made a horrible screech. I almost hit it. It almost fell over.

I saw a flash of gauze, then a curved black talon. If I'd been wearing short sleeves, the talons would have sliced my skin open. White face. Feathers. A beak that looked like a hooked nose.

The barn owl flapped its one healthy wing and opened its beak repeatedly, making no noise.

"What do you want, a dead mouse?"

Maybe Jack had forgotten to feed it. But I didn't know how to feed owls, and he could probably take my finger off with that nose-like beak.

I wished I could feed him, but I had nothing to offer.

His large dark eyes stared at me. I stared back. I felt I could see *all* owls in their roundness.

All the owls we couldn't feed.

"Owl," I said. "I'm sorry."

His black eyes stared on. Then blinked. He was hungry, I felt sure.

But in the few seconds before he scrambled off my arm again, landing awkwardly on the wooden crossbar, I wanted to believe he forgave me.

THAT WAS THE night I burst from a dream about guinea pigs and thought the forest was groaning. The wind was so fierce it snatched wet clothes off the wooden crossbar. I saw a shirt lifted and speared onto a nearby branch, where it dangled and flapped. I saw bags of dinner rolls flung into the dark, hairbrushes and flip-flops fly off and disappear.

It was the night Rafe's sleeping bag got so soaked his feet were sloshing around when he woke up, and the night two fools who hadn't put their phones in plastic found that the rain had turned them to slivers of scrap metal. I won't name names, other than to say, Low and Juicy.

It was the night the trees fell.

The force of the storm scared us. We huddled together as close as we could, balanced on the edges of platforms and ladders. In the jittery leaps of our flashlight spots we saw three trees fall one after another, dominoes. They fell at the other side of the yard, across the poison lake—a spindly one first, so thin we were surprised it had the weight to topple the others. The second and third fell after, till they were a blurred pile on the ground.

Near the true lake, trees also fell. In the morning we would see them atop the water, sinking. Their branches sagged, humped in the middle and trailing at the ends.

But firmly anchored by the village in the canopy—older and on higher ground—our own trees still stood strong.

AFTER THE RAIN stopped, it took three days for the flood-waters to recede.

On the first day a seaplane landed on the lake, the first I'd seen in real life. We watched men in blue uniforms get out and stand on the floats. Then we saw Alycia, saved.

She was wrapped in a blanket and wore big rubber boots. Her parents went out to meet her in the rowboat, since the dock was still submerged. The boathouse was waterlogged, with planks separating from the walls, warping out over the risen waters like the lifted hem of a skirt.

Alycia stepped into the boat, and the men in blue uniforms talked to the father while the mother fussed over her. Alycia gazed over her mother's head and waved at us lazily.

"They all made it," said David. "Every last jerkoff on that yacht." But he was smiling.

Actually, he looked radiant with relief.

"A fishing boat sank," said Jen. She was a newshound.

"And that cruise ship," said Low. "No death toll. *Yet.*"

Coming back across the lake in the boat, Alycia stood at the prow. She never sat down in boats—always stood. Her father rowed. Her mother looked up at her adoringly.

Later the three of them drove away from the great house in a tractor. Its big tires churned up slurries of mud and raised surges of red-brown water beside them like moving walls. In that way they made their sluggish progress down the flooded drive. And out of view.

Alycia hadn't wanted to go with them, said David— rumor had it they'd bribed her. Those parents had paid her cold, hard cash to let them take her home.

But his relief lasted.

ON THE SECOND day it was discovered that the twins were missing. Their parents hadn't noticed before, figuring they were with us. The mother's bottom lip was so chewed up from the Ecstasy it had swollen halfway down her chin.

Jack and Shel went looking and found Kay. She was sleeping in the fishing shed, surrounded by small rodent skeletons and junk-food wrappers. It was curious, Jack said: the skeletons were fresh.

As far as we knew, she was a picky eater who usually

insisted on white bread with cold cuts. On the other hand, her mouth was smeared with what looked a lot like dried blood. She smelled rancid.

Don't ask, was our approach. We marched her back to her parents.

There was no sign of her sister.

ON THE THIRD day hundreds of dying fish lay flapping on what used to be the lawn, an enormous mudflat interrupted by islands of bush. Jack and Shel splashed desperately back and forth from the mud to the real lake, carrying buckets of fishes. It was a race against time, so some of us helped them.

For those that died before they could be saved, the boys dug a mass grave. They piled the fish bodies inside it and conducted a funeral service, with readings from Jack's Bible.

"My peace I give you," read Jack sadly. "Do not let your hearts be troubled. Do not be afraid."

Shel had made a sign. His verse was written on it in block letters. He held it up in front of his chest for us to see.

ARE NOT FIVE SPARROWS SOLD FOR TWO PENNIES? AND YET NOT ONE OF THEM IS FORGOTTEN BY GOD.

We found a blow-up raft snagged in a clump of reeds in a cove of the lake. One of the flimsy rafts you use in a pool, yellow and muddy. On it lay a small man.

He had a gaunt face and wore only a pair of cargo shorts, exposing a scrawny chest and stringy legs.

He seemed to be asleep.

"Is he dead?" asked Juice.

"Nah. Chest is moving," said Sukey.

Next to me Jack cocked his head thoughtfully and tapped the shoulder bag where his picture Bible was. He'd gotten fond of it—carried it everywhere and flipped through it so often it was getting shabby. He'd done the same with his first copy of the *Frog and Toad Treasury*. Read it into rags.

"They found a guy in some reeds in my book! A baby, though. They brought him to the princess of Egypt," he told us.

"No princess of Egypt here," said Sukey. "No princess of anything."

"Alycia was the closest thing we had," said Rafe. "But she fucked off."

"What should we do with him?"

Low leaned down and poked his arm. The small man stirred, opened his eyes and did a double-take, startled by the ring of us standing around.

"Um hi?" he said. Sounded dazed.

"I'm Val," said Val, unexpectedly friendly. "Hi."

She took to the small man instantly.

"Be careful," whispered Dee. "Could be a pedophile. A molester!"

"Not a molester," objected the small man. He raised his hands, palms up. "No molesting."

"Dee?" said Sukey. "Try not to be an assface, for once."

"I'm Burl," said the small man. "Almost drowned, I think. Man. I'm *starving*."

"Energy bar?" said Val, who kept them on her person for sustenance while climbing. She slipped it out of a cargo pocket and handed it over. Burl gobbled it, ravenous.

"You live around here?" asked Terry.

Burl nodded, used his non-eating hand to wave around.

"Forest?" asked Val.

He nodded.

"Homeless, you mean?" said Dee.

"Forest," he repeated, his mouth full. "Was kayaking. It flipped. Then the storm . . ." He shook his head, swallowed and shoved the rest of the energy bar in his mouth.

"Whatevs," said Sukey.

"S'OK," said Val. "Leave him to me."

The rest of us went back to our phones and foraging. That was how we subsisted: trips to the house for water and food and recharging.

The next time I saw Burl he was climbing a tree with Val. He was no slouch, either. That small man could climb.

By and by I went to the house to use a toilet and had to thread my way through a crowd of parents. There were state troopers in the foyer.

"Eve!" yelled someone.

My mother.

"Jack having fun?" she asked.

Fun?

Turned out what she really wanted was for me to fill her glass. "Two fingers of the bourbon," she said. "Orange label. Neat."

I took the empty glass from her, purely to avoid a discussion, and then set it on the sink counter while I leisurely showered. There was still some warm water—a marvel.

As I was coming out of the bathroom she cornered me in the hallway. On her way to the liquor cabinet, likely.

"Where did you put my drink, Eve?"

"Shouldn't you be thinking about your nine-year-old son instead of your next cocktail? Honestly."

"Don't be ridiculous," she said. "I know he's safe with you. Mature beyond your years."

"Oh please."

"Even your kindergarten teacher said you were extremely precocious. Mentally *and* emotionally. They wanted to put you in fourth grade! When you were six years old!"

"You're flattering me to try to avoid responsibility? That's low." I pushed past her.

But at the end of the hall, lurking behind a bust of Susan B. Anthony, was Terry.

He'd witnessed the whole exchange.

EVERYTHING WAS TOO wet for a campfire that night, but Rafe still longed for flames. Wanted to toast the fact that he'd made it to the Final Two.

The game was down to him and Sukey.

So we stood around a grill he'd set up in the greenhouse. Its roof had been falling in even before the storm and now was mostly holes.

He burned something that looked suspiciously like sticks of furniture, and on the two-burner camp stove we boiled water and cooked ramen from packets. We ate it while playing music on David's puck-shaped speaker.

By the time Val and Burl showed up we were sharing cans of the parents' beer.

Burl was fully dressed. Val's clothes, maybe.

"We saw something," said Burl.

"A vision? I've been having those," said Low.

"We saw a bush," said Val.

"Whoa," said Sukey. "Stop the presses."

"Not sure what species, actually," reflected Burl. "It had these bright-orange flowers."

Val echoed. "Orange flowers."

"We went to survey the trees. See how many had come down. Then we saw the bush. Thing was, there were bugs swarming above it. Huge swarm of mosquitoes. Whining. I've never seen mosquitoes swarm like that," said Burl.

He paused, but it felt like he wanted to say more.

"OK," said Sukey. "Uh-huh?"

"I think we need to take off. Get out of here."

"Here where?" asked Terry. "These United States?"

"Maybe he's got a compound," said Jen, hopefully.

"Please," said Dee. "He's *homeless*." She squirted hand sanitizer on her arms.

"Get away from the house," said Burl. "The standing water. Your parents, too. I heard something about an MDMA episode . . . ? They don't seem, uh . . . well equipped."

"Damn, Burl," said Sukey. "That's not new information. But thanks for the moral support."

"Only two of us have driver's licenses," said Rafe, almost apologetically. "Two cars can't carry us all."

"I can drive," said Burl.

We looked at each other by the light of the flames.

"If one of us drove the van . . ." said Low.

"Where would we go?" asked Jen. "And what would we do when we got there?"

"Trouble's coming," said Burl.

The way he said it, somehow, it sounded real. It sounded like he *knew* something.

"Trouble's not already here?" said Sukey.

"Maybe it's a *plague*," said Jack.

"A plague?" asked Dee, and stopped rubbing sanitizer on herself. "Bacterial? *Viral?* What plague?"

"I say hell yeah," said Sukey. "Let's book."

"Come on," said Dee. "We're going to do what some homeless guy says?"

"Not homeless," said Burl. "Groundskeeper. Live in a shack. Heated."

"You're the *yard*man?" said Sukey.

"The one who drove Alycia to live with the statutory rapist?" asked Jen.

Burl's jaw dropped. He shook his head. "She said she needed *asthma* medicine!"

"There are plagues in my book," said Jack.

"Eve. Tell your baby brother," said Sukey, and crushed a beer can underfoot. "The only people who take the Bible literally are Alabama inbreds. And wife-beaters in Tennessee."

"Your family's not even Christian, Jack," said Jen. "Eve told me. And your storybook's not a user's manual."

"Ease off my brother," I said.

"They say God in the book," said Jack. "But me and Shel figured it out. God's a code word. We figured it out!"

"Do tell," said Jen.

"They say God but they mean *nature*."

Shel signed.

"And we believe in nature," Jack interpreted.

"OK," said Terry. "How about Isaac and Abraham? Was it *nature* that told a guy he had to knife his son to death?"

Shel signed a bunch more. He stood up, agitated.

"Nature gets misinterpreted," said Jen. "Shel says."

"Plus it's a story," added Jack. "Things are *symbols*."

I was impressed.

"Point is," Burl interrupted. "Point is, it doesn't feel right here. I know this place. We need to get away."

"We *could*, like . . ." began Dee, then trailed off, hesitant.

"What?" said Sukey. "Spit it out."

". . . *tell* them? Tell the parents?"

Rafe shook his head. Juicy chortled.

"What, tell them a homeless guy said that it's time to go?" said Low.

"Not homeless," said Burl, quiet. "Just saying. Not a homeless molester."

JACK'S WORRY WAS the animals. If they couldn't come with us, he and Shel couldn't leave. The animals needed protection.

The little boys were stubborn, and I finally broke down: what if we packed their animals into the van? Rafe and David had full licenses, but Sukey and I could also drive, in a pinch. We had learner's permits.

Last was the problem of our destination. We had to reveal our home bases, choose the best prospect.

It turned out Juicy's place took the prize: a mansion in Westchester County. He'd once muttered "north of Harlem"—probably trying to maintain his street cred.

Which was imaginary.

He lived in a ten-bedroom house in Rye.

TERRY WAS THE spokesperson, as usual. We went with him to the great house when we were finished packing up the vehicles. No parents had even noticed.

David's mother lay on a couch in the library with a cold compress on her forehead. Other mothers and fathers milled around aimlessly, like robots with no programming.

"Excuse me? Attention?" said Terry.

No one listened.

"Use this," said Sukey.

She handed him a rape whistle. It was the one the parents blew for dinner, but none of us had ever touched it. So when it suddenly shrilled, the parents gathered. Puzzled and annoyed.

The David mother leapt up from the couch.

"Amy? Is it *Amy*?"

"No," said David.

She subsided again.

Terry mentioned the fact that the house had two gaping holes in it, including one that had wrecked our sleeping quarters. The yard was a muddy waste surrounded by fallen trees. The basement was two feet deep in toxic floodwater, and there were serious electrical hazards. The tap water might be unsafe to drink. The power was still out. All in all, our vacation paradise had turned into hell. And the bugs were getting bad, he added. They might carry disease.

Could we please leave?

It sounded reasonable to me.

But the parents shook their heads.

"Even if little Amy wasn't missing, we need to fix the damage or we won't get back our deposit," said a mother.

"If the management company hires their *own* contractors, the surcharge will be highway robbery," said a father.

"Then there's the breach of the lease agreement. What was the penalty, again?"

"Seventy thousand, I believe."

"At least."

"Leaving right now is, frankly, unacceptable."

The yacht parents wouldn't have given a shit, I thought. For them seventy grand was just a quick, private dinner flight to Paris.

BEFORE WE LEFT we carved our initials into the waterlogged posts of the Ark. I felt melancholy saying goodbye to the house: it was flooded, cold and dark and boarded up, but once it had been the site of splendid parties.

More than a century ago, said Terry, empire builders and criminals, famous artists and actors and ass-kissers had floated in their finery beneath the Roosevelt chandelier.

And in the future, he said, maybe a new generation of partyers would arrive. Much like us, but strangers to us forever, they'd look upon our names and wonder who we'd been.

"Or after us there won't be anyone," said Rafe. "Maybe we're the last."

"The oceans are rising," said David.

"The plagues are coming," piped up Jack.

"This forest, too, will fall," said Jen.

They didn't know if they were joking.

BURL VOLUNTEERED TO drive the van, with the little boys and their zoo in the back. I still don't know how they lured the barn owl in, but when I slid into the front seat I turned around and saw it behind us, perched on a branch stuck between two cages.

Looking out the window as we pulled around the crescent onto the straightaway, I spied some parents running out the front door, waving their arms. Not my parents, of course.

I thought: Enh, they'll get used to it. Children grow up. Children leave.

They'll find us, I thought. When we want them to.

There was standing water on the dirt drive that wound through the woods to the edge of the property. Ahead of us a car sank two wheels into the mud. Juicy and Val got out and shoved a branch beneath a tire, but the engine revved and revved. Burl had to jump out to help.

Waiting for him to finish, I saw some parents beginning to gain on us—three. Running, since we'd hidden the keys to the cars we'd left behind. We'd text their location from a safe distance.

It was highly unusual to see a parent run.

Several of us were transfixed by the sight.

But then Burl got in again and we were off, in the lead. Rust-red water surged up around the van, but we had momentum. We didn't sink beneath the waves.

5

TWENTY MINUTES OUT our progress was halted. Across the road more trees had collapsed—recently, it looked like. They'd taken a power line down with them, and it was popping and sparking across the top of the leafy mass.

Rerouting, I texted to the group, and pulled my finger around on the map app.

But the alternate routes were all in red, with multiple hazard signs on them.

We got out of our cars, except for Jack and Shel who wanted to check on the animals, and clustered on the road fiddling with our map apps.

None of the routes looked promising.

Some of us kicked at tires. We'd be damned if we were

going back to the parents. We'd feel like losers, retreating with our tails between our legs.

More importantly, we just didn't want to.

"I do know one place," said Burl, after a while.

"A place," said Val, encouraging.

"A farm," he said. "Fields. A barn. It's inland. Safer. Farther from the ocean."

He said there was plenty of straw we could sleep on in the barn. That sounded uncomfortable. Plus flies, roaches, spiders, and possibly fire ants.

At Juicy's mansion there were memory-foam mattresses, king-sized. And an infinity pool.

"Are there, like, cows on that farm?" asked Rafe. "They depress me. Doomed. *Zero* exceptions. It's either a bolt shot through your head when you're two or they let you live till you're five. Make you a breeder and kidnap all your babies. Suck out the milk that was meant for them. And after that you die."

"I didn't *realize* you were vegan," said Sukey, slightly sneering.

"Whose barn *is* it?" asked Dee.

"Rich lady's," said Burl. "She's a hobby farmer. I do maintenance for her. Not there now. Lives in TriBeCa."

The map app gave us a clear path when Burl entered the address—not that the app could be trusted. It also wanted us to levitate across the sparking power line.

"It wouldn't be for long," added Sukey. "Someone will

clear these trees, won't they? Then we get out of the barn and head to Juicy's badass crib. OK?"

Juicy preened.

In the van Burl reversed quickly and accelerated back up the road. He liked to drive boldly.

There was a bad smell.

"The bunny made a mess," admitted Jack.

"Son, that's not rabbit turds," said Burl. He had the air of one who knew.

"So did the possum. And the skunk. They're scared."

"The *skunk*?" said Burl.

"A *skunk's* back there?" I echoed.

"She's a nice skunk," said Jack.

"So, I've been wondering," I said to him. "To save the animals, wouldn't you have to get two of each? Isn't it a problem, down the road, if you only save one?"

Jack looked at me, amazed.

"Evie," he said, in a reproachful tone. "Are you kidding? We're not the *only* ones."

"The only ones what?"

"Collecting. There are lots of others doing it."

"How do you know?"

"You've got to have *faith*, Evie."

Burl and I shared a sidelong look.

"One thing's for sure. The deaf kid's amazing," said Burl to me under his breath. "I never saw a pro trapper as fast as him."

"You used *traps*?" I asked Jack.

I'd pictured him and Shel with arms spread wide, animals strolling in. Hadn't questioned it.

That was how distracted I'd been.

"Havaharts," he said. "The biggest one fits a raccoon. We got them from the toolshed. Evie! No animal was hurt! The Havaharts work really good."

"I guess they do," said Burl. He shook his head. "A skunk, right here. With us. Well, damn."

He drove less boldly after that.

THE BARN WAS painted red, and next to it was a white cottage with ivy growing up to the roof. There was an old metal grain silo looming. Together they nearly looked picturesque.

Best, no trees were down. That made it feel peaceful. A haven, almost. No sound but a breeze in the woods across the field, and in the distance a siren.

At the edge of the field there were three donkeys grazing. I pointed out some sheep. Six or seven.

"They're not sheep. They're goats," Jack said.

"How do you tell the difference?"

"Goat tails go up, Evie! Sheep tails go down."

Behind the cottage Burl showed us a generator, which he connected so the refrigerator would get cold. We'd snagged some cartons of milk and sticks of butter. Inside the barn we saw two rows of stalls and a hayloft, some dusty farm machinery. We climbed the ladder to the hayloft and found bales of hay. As promised.

There were a couple of all-terrain vehicles, which Low and Juicy jumped on. Electric, with push-button ignitions. Dee scolded them into wearing helmets she found hanging on pegs, and they went swerving across the pasture.

A few of us hung out in the cottage kitchen, where we could plug in our phones. The signal wasn't strong enough for voice calls—the parents' scolding voicemails came through patchy, which was just fine—but we could browse.

We read how the storm had flooded the subway tunnels in New York, and in Boston the river had overflowed its banks. Downed power lines electrocuted drivers, and cars and garbage cans and pets had been swept away down streets that looked like rushing rivers.

We watched video of collapsing houses.

"Don't you think they just, like, rerun the same footage from every hurricane before?" asked Sukey.

Usually it was of Florida or Louisiana or other places none of us lived. Now it claimed to be of closer locations. Pine trees whipping around instead of palms.

Riots, they said. Looting. States of emergency. The president had promised some money.

"One day there won't be any money left," pronounced Terry.

"Even the apps will stop working," added Sukey.

We were downcast, there in the cottage. Downcast and uncertain. Relieved to be where we were, for sure.

But out there, beyond our field of view, the options were shrinking. Choices were being removed.

I slumped against the counter with my phone. On Instagram James had posted curated pictures of his ocean misadventure.

"Take a look," I said.

There he was in a selfie, bare-chested in front of a stormy sky and perfectly filtered. One arm was raised to the heavens, displaying his well-molded pecs. The arm was holding an orange flag with a black square and circle on it.

#SOS, said his comment. He was smiling.

There was Alycia in profile, a white, slit-skirted dress flying out behind her and exposing her slender legs.

#goddess.

There were two faces pressed cheek to cheek and looking at the camera: an overly tanned older man, grimacing and shiny, and the trophy wife. They were holding up champagne flutes in hands loaded down with bling.

#ilovemyshipwreckedparents.

"Hashtag asskiss," said Rafe.

"Parents? She's not even his mother!" said Sukey.

"Unless she had him when she was three," said Jen.

I quit the app.

"Good climbing trees off the east pasture," said Burl to Val.

"Good climbing trees," said Val.

I followed the two of them through the door, stood in the cottage garden under an arched wooden trellis with small roses growing over it. Watched them walk past a fenced enclosure where some vegetables were growing—tall rows of corn, dark clumps I'd learn later were kale and chard. Bees circled and grapevines climbed the fences, hanging in sweeps of green.

As the tree climbers struck out together across the field, I felt surprisingly fond of them. Two small figures, a little hunched over, who might have been related. Raised close together in some monkey tribe. Humble, efficient clamberers, at home up in the canopy.

We'd made it to the farm, and it was all because of Burl. Out there the roads had turned into dead ends. Without him we would have driven and driven and got nowhere. Only Burl, Burl and the spark of energy that was his knowledge, had found us a refuge.

JACK AND I were setting down animal cages in the barn when a car horn honked. I went out the creaky wooden door to behold a dreaded thing: a mother.

The fat one.

She got out of her car and stood there, hands on hips, red in the face. She was wearing a long, flowing dress, as though she'd raided the peasant mother's closet.

"*Sukey!*" she bellowed. "*Sukey!*"

So she *was* Sukey's mother, after all.

Well, Sukey had bluffed her way out of that one. For a long time. No one had called her bluff, and bluffing was certainly allowed.

But now she'd lost. Miserably.

IT TURNED OUT the fat mother had used her phone's location tracking to find us. The two of them yelled at each other in the yard. We weren't coming back to the house, shouted Sukey, so her mother could suck it. We'd stolen cars and had to bring them back, yelled her mother. Actual stolen property! They could report us!

In your dreams, said Sukey.

The others emerged one by one from the cottage and the barn, except for Val and Burl, who were off climbing. Juice even parked his ATV. We were pretty much there for the fat-mother show. Though also nervous. There would be repercussions.

"What are you doing here, *trespassing*?" shouted the mother. "You could be *arrested*! You want to land in *juvie*?"

"Oh please," said Sukey. "You know I already got a full ride to Brown."

"You think that gives you *immunity*?"

"We know the owner, so yeah," said Sukey, stretching the truth. "It's all good."

"Horse pucky," said her mother.

"We do," insisted Sukey. "A hobby farmer from SoHo!"

"TriBeCa, actually," said Terry.

"Then let me talk to her," said the mother.

"Not here now," said Sukey. "*Obviously.*"

"I worry," said the mother. Her voice changed. It got quavery. "We're *worried* about you."

This was something we hadn't suspected.

"Huh," said Sukey. Belligerent. Disbelieving.

"Oh no," said the mother, and doubled over.

"*What*," said Sukey, arms crossed.

"Oh no. My water broke!"

We all stared. I think I can fairly say the general thought was, *What the fuck.*

"Are you making this up?" said Sukey. "It's supposed to be another month!"

The fat mother wasn't so fat.

Or at least, the fatness was temporary.

We saw the so-called water, then. We saw it and we didn't like it.

"Oh, *oh*," moaned Sukey's mother. "Contraction."

"Goddamn," said Sukey. "Goddammit! You mess up *every*thing! Why did you have to come *here*? *Jesus!*"

"You have to drive me. *Oh!* You have to. I can't drive now. You *have to drive me Sukey!*"

Sukey looked around at us. Despairing.

"You can always come back," I suggested.

But it didn't have the ring of feasibility.

Sukey trudged into the barn, came out with her duffel. She looked down at the ground. Shook her head in defeat.

Then they got into the car, the mother staggering.

And Sukey drove away.

It was only a matter of time until another parent showed up. We should leave too, said Rafe—put our phones in airplane mode and clear out.

He barely had the heart to celebrate his victory. The game was done, but its ending hadn't left any of us happy.

So we gathered around a campfire when darkness fell trying to find a route to Juicy's mansion for the morning. Even our former route, with the sparking power lines and downed trees, didn't come up.

Juicy wanted to smoke the parents' pot, but we voted against it. We had to keep our wits about us, said Terry.

He tried to drape his arm over Jen's shoulders, but she shrugged it off. Irritated.

"They wouldn't resort to force, would they?" said Rafe.

"They can't outsmart us," said Terry.

"Don't be an idiot. If Sukey's mother could do it, then so can anyone," said Jen. "She's borderline retarded."

Technology was a bitch. Short of disabling or ditching the phones, David said, we couldn't isolate perfectly.

"Maybe we stay here even *if* they know," said Dee. "They're not going to call the police, are they?"

"We're not a priority," said David. "Plus they're still looking for Amy."

We noticed Val at the edge of the circle of light. And Burl. They'd come back.

"Went up a hill," said Burl.

"Hill," nodded Val. "Went up it."

"Hill?" asked Low. "There's a *hill* around here?"

"Couple miles. Cell tower on the ridge," said Burl. "Solid reception. Talked to the owner of this place. She said to pass along some ground rules, if we stay."

Val stepped nearer the fire and lifted her arms, pulling up the sleeves of her sweatshirt. We saw words written on the skin in small letters. Ballpoint. She squinted at her right arm first.

"First rules. Uh. She's the owner. So we gotta do what she says. And also respect her."

"But how would she know if we didn't?" asked Juice.

Val shrugged. "Don't make noise on the weekend."

"In case the other city people make it up here," Burl explained. "The weekenders tend to want peace and quiet."

"Next," read Val, "respect your elders."

"Huh. Easier said than done," said Rafe.

"Hey, I count," said Burl. "Just try to respect *me*."

"No breaking the law," said Val, and switched from her right arm to her left. "And no sex."

"*What?*" squealed Jen.

"Puritanical," said Terry.

"Frigid," said Juicy.

"Disrespect. You already broke rule two," said Jen.

"The other ones are, don't steal her stuff, tell her what's up if she checks in, and don't try to hook up with the neighbors' kids. Or steal the neighbors' stuff."

"She's pretty hung up on the neighbors," said David.

"And sex," said Jen. "Why does she even care?"

"What's there to steal?" said Rafe. "Donkeys?"

"That's it," said Val, and pushed down her sleeves again. "Food, please?"

"So what's the penalty if we break the rules?" asked Dee.

"Yeah. Are there punishments?" asked Juice.

"How can she punish us if she's not here?" said Jen.

"Surveillance?" asked David.

"Hey, Evie!" called Jack. He'd just come out of the barn, Shel tagging along behind him. "We took the bandage off. He flies!"

A blur of bird flew away from them onto the roof. It landed and perched on the peak.

Fast healing, was what struck me first.

What struck me second was, maybe the bandage had actually been the culprit.

I mean, they were little kids. Not vets.

But I didn't say it. Of course not. Jack was my boy.

"That's amazing!" I said, instead.

David's phone dinged.

"Huh. The parents are getting sick," he said, reading.

"Sick how?" I asked.

"Fever and chills. Headaches."

We looked at Burl.

"Could be anything," he said modestly.

"Or it could be a plague," said Dee.

We sat there, saying little.

"Food, please," repeated Val.

"Pot's on the stove," said Jen.

Val and Burl headed off.

The rest of us were silent. I hadn't taken the plague seriously. For me it had mostly been an excuse to get out. But now?

Now I wasn't so sure.

I wasn't sure what we owed the parents, either. Were they desperate? Did they need help?

No one wanted to talk about it. But we were thinking.

Then David's text alert dinged again.

"Huh," he said.

"What?" asked Jen.

"My mother says not to come back now."

"What?" asked Rafe.

"She says it could be catching."

We sat there in the flicker and glow. I marveled: the parents, caught in a selfless gesture.

I almost wanted to thank them.

RAFE PUT OUT the fire after a while, and that was when, walking back to the barn, I saw the sky and pointed. We stopped and gazed upward.

"What the *hell*," said Jen.

There were shifting waves of light above us, green and purple. Bands and rays. Beautiful.

"Psychedelic," said Juice.

"Impossible," said David. "Isn't it?"

"It's the aurora," said Jack.

"*Aurora borealis*," said Terry.

"I thought those were at the North Pole," objected Jen.

"And South," said Rafe.

"Yeah. Penguins can see them," said Jack.

"My relative saw them. When he conquered the Siberian wastes, one thousand years ago," said Low. "His name was Genghis Khan."

Old banana.

"Where are we, anyway?" asked Jen.

Burl was chewing on a stick of something. Beef jerky, maybe. Or red licorice.

"Pennsylvania," he said. "Near the state line."

"Did the storm do this?" asked Jen.

"Is it a sign?" asked Low.

"Doubt it," said Burl, still chewing. "Technically, it's magnetic activity on the sun's surface. A solar maximum, maybe."

He was pretty smart, for a yardman.

Long after the others had slipped into their sleeping bags and tents, I lay out in the grass and watched the green waves. Finally had my alone time.

It was the best light show ever.

Genghis Khan had seen the waves, if you believed Low. The Inuit had seen them. Walruses and penguins. And now I was seeing them. But who would see them later?

I thought of sparkling platforms in space, silver airships

moving in front of the billions of stars. I thought of vines that grew over the ruins of buildings and monuments.

I felt an itch and thought, Is there a tick crawling on me? Right this minute? Burrowing into my skin?

And then I thought, Wait. Forget the tick. Why are we always complaining? We get to be alive.

6

IN THE DREAM I was happy to see Sukey's face. *Dear Sukey,* I thought, half-asleep. Our ringleader. Dear ringleader. I missed her already. There was brightness around the face, and prickly things stuck into me. I had to get the sharp things out.

They were pieces of straw, because I was in the hayloft and had rolled off my sleeping pad.

"Fuck," said the face.

So it was really her.

I scrambled up. She knelt next to me, puffing from climbing the loft ladder. Her flashlight was blinding.

"We couldn't get anywhere," she panted. "Not even back to the house. The bridge over that stream we crossed coming out? It was caved in! There was, like, half of it left. I tried all the routes. But she won't walk anymore. I had to practically carry her in."

"Is she still having a baby?"

What can I say, I was half-asleep.

"She's downstairs. What am I going to do?"

"What happened to your stepfather? Where's *he*?"

"He's not my stepfather."

"Whatever, Suke. The baby's father."

"They broke up. She found out he hooked up with someone else."

"What, in the Ecstasy deal?"

"Nah. Before the summer. Whatever. He said he never wanted the baby. Took off for the city when they were buying supplies for the storm. She was going on about it in the car, but I was just like, I *told* you he was an asshole."

"We have to call 911."

"I called from the road. But I couldn't get through."

"Keep trying."

"But the contractions—they're, like, often."

I reached over and poked Rafe. He grunted and woke up. Then I poked Jen.

"Stand at that loft door till you get three bars," I told her, bossy. "We need an ambulance. Or medevac."

The three of us put on our headlamps and followed Sukey down the ladder. I heard the others stirring. A couple of donkeys had wandered in.

On the ground floor was Sukey's mother. She sat on

a blanket, her legs sticking out in front of her and spread open.

"Thank you, sweet Jesus, for sending that long dress," murmured Rafe.

The mother was rocking back and forth, moaning.

"We need to get her in the cottage," said Sukey. "Don't we? It's cleaner there."

The mother shook her head. "I'm not moving," she said. And moaned again. "I'm *not*. I'm *not moving!*"

"Put her in that stall," called Dee from the loft. "The one with no hay on the floor. I was going to sleep there so I scrubbed it down with bleach. But then I came up here anyway. It still smelled *disgusting.*"

SUKEY AND I pulled the blanket with the mother sitting on it. We held the two leading corners, the way you drag heavy furniture on a towel or rug. We had to steer around a donkey that wouldn't move.

The mother swayed backward and fell over like a sack.

"I'll get Burl," said Val, swinging down from a rafter. Everyone but the little boys was awake by then.

We sat the mother up again when we had the blanket straight, and then we leaned her against the back wall of the stall. Her eyes were closed. She breathed noisily.

"Pillows?" said Sukey.

"Maybe some ice. Look how she's sweating," said Rafe.

"We don't have ice," said David.

"I'm sleeping outside," said Juicy, lugging his sleeping bag across the floor. It swept up pieces of straw, dust, and probably donkey manure.

"Me too," said Low. "This shit's hairy."

"How'd *you* get born?" yelled Jen, from the hay door. "You think it was a holy stork? All white with virgin choirs singing a hymn? As it flew by and dropped you in a golden crib?"

"It was a vag," said Sukey.

"Was not," said Juicy. "I was a C-section."

"Hold music!" shouted Jen from the loft. "I got the hold music!"

Sukey perked up at that. Until her mother screamed.

And Burl came in. Behind him was a small group of bedraggled people we'd never seen before. Four of them. Beards and greasy hair. Long backpacks loomed up over their shoulders, and as they got nearer, I smelled feet and armpits.

Three men and one woman, if I was pegging the sexes right. Only the beards tipped me off. Their skin and hair and clothing were all the same color: dirt.

"Who are *these* jokers?" asked Sukey.

"Came off the Appalachian Trail. They're trail angels," said Burl.

"That sounds gay," said Juice.

"I warned you not to say *gay* like that," said Rafe. "Now I have to rain hellfire down on your stupid head."

"What's a trail angel?" asked Jen.

"They go to spots on the trail and leave water and food there," said Burl. "Charity. You know, for long-distance hikers. The ones that hike the whole two thousand miles."

"Someone walks for two thousand miles?" asked Sukey.

"Thru-hikers. Most trail angels just leave stuff where they can drive to. These ones were more hardcore," said Burl.

"We were on a weeklong backpack for food delivery," said one of the men. "Just finishing up when the storm hit."

"Hey. Anyone with a medical background?" asked Burl, turning to the group. "We have a woman in labor here."

"Here. Name's Luca. Had some EMT training," said one of the angels.

Sukey beckoned him over. Her mother screamed again—less of a scream than a roar.

"I'll do what I can," said Luca, and swung his pack off his back. The other angels were putting their packs down too. I might have asked Burl how he'd picked them to join us, but I was too relieved to think of it.

"Sukey! I need Sukey!" grunted the mother.

"I'll be back," said Sukey. "Just gotta wash my hands."

"What's our address?" called Jen from above. "I got someone! I got an operator!"

Burl scrambled up the ladder and took the phone.

"It's a dirt road," he said, and gave some directions. "The nearest town? Uh, so. It's in the middle of nowhere. But east of our location is a town called Alpha. West is Bethlehem."

Luckily Jack was a heavy sleeper.

MOST OF US left the barn then, claiming the scene was none of their business. I didn't think it was mine either, but Jen and I had to stay, because Sukey asked us to.

No ambulance ever showed.

When the top of the baby's head was emerging and angels were murmuring words of encouragement, I stepped out of the stall. The mother was squirming and growling. I wanted to look at anything else so I chose one of Jack's brown mammals, maybe a groundhog. I squatted next to its cage and tried to see its face, but it had its back to me. I stared at its fur. We were both mammals, I thought.

So we had that in common.

The baby wailed.

That was how Sukey got a sister. But her mother wouldn't stop bleeding.

And so her mother died.

WE FELT FAR away for a while. In shock, I guess. On the one hand, we hardly knew Sukey's mother. Along with the rest of the parents, she'd pretty much gotten on our nerves. Though I didn't want to dwell on that.

On the other hand, she was dead.

Sukey hadn't *liked* her mother either, as such, but this went way beyond.

Others must have cleaned up afterward. All I saw was

a red-soaked towel mounded in a bucket. Jen and I stayed with our little brothers, sitting and holding them. Juicy and Low came in once, looked, and left, slumping and kicking at straw as they went.

Jack and I watched as the barn owl flew over us and perched on the open stall door above the mother's body. It was covered in a white sheet from the cottage bed.

The owl stayed. Keeping watch.

For the first time since we'd come to the country I felt unsteady. I couldn't tell if it was fear or confusion.

"Evie," said Jack. "Is she really dead?"

"She is, Jack, I'm afraid," I said. No way to sugarcoat it.

"Why did she die, Evie?"

"She lost a lot of blood, you see."

He started to cry, and I pulled him onto my lap and rocked back and forth. Half for him, half for me.

I tried to calm myself by picturing everyday, organized systems: my room at home, chest of drawers, mirror, closet. The hangers in the closet, the sweaters folded in the drawers. I counted them and cataloged their different colors. I tried to remember how the periodic table went. They'd made us memorize it in chemistry, but that had been fall semester. Ages ago. *1 H: Hydrogen. 2 He: Helium. 3 Li: Lithium. 4 Be: Beryllium* . . . then I drew a blank.

So I ran through the list of irregular verbs and their conjugations that we'd had to memorize in French. I preferred French to chemistry.

Être. Je suis. I am. Tu es. You are. Familiar form.

SUKEY SAT BESIDE her dead mother all night holding the baby. When morning came the angels convinced her to bathe it, and they steered her out of the barn and into the cottage.

I gave Jack and Shel a task to distract them: find the goats, make sure they were still around. We didn't want to lose any, I said.

Then I went to the mother's car, parked at a hasty angle behind the ones we'd driven in, and popped the trunk. There was a bag of baby clothes, with a bottle and a packet of minuscule diapers. She'd had it all ready, I thought, and felt a wave fold over me.

She'd wanted to care for her infant. And now she never would.

Sukey dressed the baby in a cotton sleeper with feet attached.

I tried to call her stepfather using the mother's cell— Sukey nodded mechanically when I pointed to his name under Contacts—but there was no answer. Mailbox full.

So we had two problems: how to feed the baby, and what to do with the mother's body.

One of the angels had a bag of powdered milk, but that would make the baby sick. Another angel—a biologist who'd been surveying birds along the trail and joined the others when the storm hit—warned against it.

We didn't have a mother, so we needed infant formula.

Burl set off in a car to look for it. There was a gas station convenience store, he said, about five miles away. They might have some.

David and Terry helped wrap the mother in a shroud made of sheets. The angels conferred in hushed tones in a corner of the barn, near an empty chicken coop.

I snuck up and crouched behind a donkey to listen.

"She's just a kid," I heard one whisper. "Trying to take care of a newborn, for Chrissake. We can't put it on her."

". . . a suggestion. And let her say yes."

"Or no."

"Burial here isn't legal."

"That's why I said fire."

"But burial can be undone. When things get back under control. Fire? Not so much."

"Maybe we wait?"

"But that could be traumatic. You know. The decomp. Could be a lot of days before we go anywhere. Weeks, even."

"The father?"

"Out of the picture. They can't raise him."

"What if they need it for an autopsy?"

"They've got bigger fish to fry. CNN said *thousands*."

Thousands of what?

THEY SENT A delegation to Sukey. I followed. She was in the cottage bedroom sitting cross-legged on the bed, the baby in her arms.

"In the Hindu tradition," began the angel woman, who

was white but had brown dreadlocks, "fire purifies and lets the soul escape the body. So they construct beautiful funeral pyres. They wrap the departed in white . . ."

Sukey stared at her. And spoke. "She wasn't a fucking Hindu."

"I didn't mean—" started the angel.

"But a pyre would be OK, I guess."

The rest of us had to collect firewood, since the pile beside the cottage wasn't enough. It took us a while to find dry kindling. Rafe was in charge of building the pyre, and we did what he said.

We were tired and sore by the time it was high enough. It was higher than our heads, on purpose. We didn't want to have a close-up view.

As the sun went down the angels carried the long white bundle from the barn to the pyre on some planks and lifted it to the top. Their hands were shaky—I remember noticing that. I was afraid they'd drop it.

While Rafe was lighting the kindling out came Sukey, still carrying the baby. Wouldn't put her down. Her cheeks were streaked with the dirty tracks of tears, but she looked straight at the mother's shroud and didn't cry again.

We had a couple of false starts: damp wood had gotten in. But in due time flames crept up. Rafe was anxious. He'd rigged a metal cage to organize the wood—the chicken coop stacked on top of a water trough—and he was worried about collapse. Every time a log or branch shifted I heard a sharp intake of breath.

The angels were more or less hippies. Because of this, probably, they couldn't help breaking into song. David had seen it coming, he said. Inevitable, agreed Terry.

First was the woman, Darla. She sang all by herself in Latin. She told us she was "offering a tribute" she knew from her youth. She'd grown up Catholic, she said. But she had gotten spiritual since then.

She had a high clear voice.

"*Ahhhhh-ve Mari-i-a,*" she sang. "*Grati-ia plena, Do-ominus tecum.*"

"The Lord is with thee," translated Terry. "Blessed art thou amongst women, and blessed is the fruit—"

Rafe dug an elbow into his ribs.

When she finished singing, the others took it up. The next song was in English. It was a sixties song about seasons turning, laughing and weeping and peace, *I swear it's not too late.* We wouldn't have sung even if we'd known the song, which we didn't. Except for Low.

We listened. For a while it was embarrassing. But gradually it wasn't.

You could almost feel love for the mother, listening to the hippies sing. Or pity that passed for love.

Or maybe was the same.

THE ANGELS DIDN'T want Sukey to see bone fragments, so they collected the ashes in a paper bag. We dug a shallow grave in the far corner of the field and buried the bag there. Then we trooped back over the meadow and dispersed.

Muscles aching from tiredness, I hauled myself up the ladder to put Jack to bed. Read him a book by flashlight. *George and Martha Tons of Fun.*

He passed out right away. My boy was even more exhausted than I was.

I sat beside his sleeping bag for a while listening to him breathe.

THAT NIGHT I thought I'd never want to eat again, but the next morning I woke up hungry. David was hungry too, so he and I made our way to the kitchen early.

Burl had gotten back with a box of infant formula and a package of diapers. He had a gash on his cheek, which Luca was dabbing with disinfectant. Darla stood at the counter and mixed formula with water.

"What happened?" I asked.

Burl flinched as Luca poked with a cotton ball. "Lawless," he said. "Lucky to get what I got."

"Lawless?" I asked.

"I locked the front gate. You can still come in by foot, but not by car."

"We're closing in on the autumnal equinox," said Darla. "Virgo and Leo are aligned. Did you all see the aurora?"

We nodded.

"Could be a major celestial event," said Darla. "A message. *Very* meaningful."

"Charged particles," said Burl. He sounded resigned. "Science. It's not anomalous. The northern lights have been sighted before in these parts. Saw them myself. Four summers ago."

I went through the fridge and the cabinets, rifling. If we had to feed the angels, I estimated we had the makings for one, maybe two more regular meals.

"Burl," I said. "What about food?"

"We're OK there," he said.

"How do you figure? We have, like, three pounds of linguini."

"And stale assorted bagels," said Darla.

She pointed to the counter. Burl had brought those too.

"I'll show you later," he said.

Jen came out of the bedroom—she'd spent the night helping Sukey with the baby—and exclaimed in relief at the bottle of formula.

"These diapers are too large," said Darla, ripping open the bag. "They're for eighteen-month-olds!"

"Gimme a break," said Burl. "They didn't have the newborn size."

I unpacked bagels and cream cheese, then yelled from the front door. The rest of us thronged in.

"Good to know they still have bagels in chaos," said Rafe.

"Goes to show. Jews *are* the chosen people," said David.

He stuffed an Everything in his mouth.

I felt a twinge of envy. There was only one Everything.

"Anti-Semite," said Jen.

"Well . . . I'm a Jew, though," said David.

"Self-hating," said Jen.

"I got them from a donut shop," said Burl. "Door open. Windows smashed in."

I grabbed a couple of bagels and set out for the barn to find Jack. The little boys were sitting on a hay bale, writing in a notebook.

Drawing near, I saw the open Bible—an illustration of loaves and fishes. The loaves looked a lot like baguettes, which I wondered if they'd eaten in ancient Judea.

Also, the fish were smiling.

"I brought you breakfast," I said.

"Thanks, Evie," said Jack. Preoccupied.

"What are you doing?"

"Decoding," he said.

"You're obsessed with that book," I said. "Honestly. It worries me."

"Don't worry, Evie," he said, and signed something to Shel, who nodded. "Shel says don't worry too."

"It's tough times, isn't it," I said.

I gave him a sideways hug before I went out again.

In the cottage kitchen Burl was being debriefed.

"What you have out there," he said, "is some folks pretty frightened. Some armed to the teeth. The road system's useless. So as far as getting to your house in Westchester"—he looked at Juicy—"it's no dice. Even if the roads were passable, we wouldn't be able to fuel up. There was a run on gas. The pumps that aren't dry are locked down by crazies. Saw a gas station with a yellow Jeep guarding the entrance. Guys holding rifles."

I gazed around. Dee looked frightened. Juice tore at a bagel with his teeth and stared at the floor, but his hands were unsteady. Rafe was attentive and thoughtful. Terry drummed his fingers on the table, anxious but not freaking out. Low's face was settling into a determined expression, like maybe it was time to summon the vengeful spirit of the Khan.

And Val—well, Val I could never read. She stood at Burl's shoulder, patting the pockets of her cargo pants until she pulled out a pocketknife.

Jen and Sukey were in the bedroom and hadn't heard any of it.

When Burl led us to the silo—Val and Rafe and me—we followed without speaking. In suspense.

The silo door had some serious locks. A rubber flap with

a high-tech keypad underneath. While Burl punched but-
tons and turned keys, I craned my neck and looked above.
It wasn't much from the outside—gray metal, with peeling
white paint and patches of rust. Went up and up and up.

Then he pushed open the door. Flicked on the lights.

Stairs spiraled along the wall to the roof. There were
shelves on the walls. And the place looked solid. Insulated,
even. Leather armchairs and carpeting. Wires running up
and down. A gun cabinet fronted in glass.

Rafe whistled through his teeth.

"We're just here for the food," said Burl.

He directed us to carry dry goods from the shelves. We
made two trips while he waited, carried eight boxes back to
the cottage. The first thing to come out of my box was a ten-
pound bag of rice. It looked like we'd be eating a lot of that.
Plus beans, canned peaches, and peanut butter.

"Go figure. You had a compound after all," said Rafe,
while we were unpacking.

"Just a custodian," said Burl. "I don't have squat,
personally."

I told Rafe I thought we should try calling 911 again for
the parents, in case they couldn't make a call.

"Sure they can make a call. The house has a landline,"
he said.

"That's cold," I said.

"May work. May not. Buried cables on the property,"
said Burl. "But once they hit the road, they go up in the air.
And a lot of *those* lines are down."

JEN'D GOTTEN RECEPTION in the hayloft before, so I sat up there on a bale and texted my parents: *How are you?* and *How sick?*

Ready to dial 911 if needed.

I got nothing.

I gazed down as the biologist talked to Jack and Shel, gesturing. I couldn't hear what he was saying, and I was looking at the tops of their heads, but after a while the boys walked to a cage and carried it out the double doors.

Then another cage and a box, till all the animals were gone. Just the aquarium and the buckets remained.

I climbed down the ladder and followed them. At the edge of the field, where a row of saplings separated the cottage garden from the pasture, the cages and boxes were lined up on the grass. The boys bent over each of them in turn.

Rabbits hopped out and scampered off. Ditto a squirrel. An orange fox, its big triangle ears tinged narrowly in black, bolted and disappeared.

The skunk box got carried farther out, and I waited nervously. But the boys trudged back across the field without incident, and the skunk's puff of a tail waved lazily as it ambled into the brush.

"How did you convince them?" I asked the biologist.

He had smooth, olive skin. For an older guy, not totally disfigured.

"I just showed them the animals were suffering."

We stood beside each other, me feeling awkward as the

boys approached. I told him my name and he told me his. Mattie. It sounded like a girl's name, I said.

He said he got that a lot. He said it'd been his nickname when he was little, and he ended up keeping it.

Jack's face was serene when he came up to me.

"Evie," he said, solemn. "The storm passed. And there's no plague here. So we had to set them free."

Up in the loft I sat at the edge of the hay door, dangling my legs off the side. The little boys made their way toward the stream that ran through the woods. Carrying fish containers.

Ding, came a text alert.

From my father.

Dengue fever, the text said.

I looked it up. *A mosquito-borne tropical disease—*

I scrambled back down the ladder.

Mattie was inspecting plants in the vegetable garden, turning over leaves and rubbing his thumb over their undersides.

"Come with me?" I said.

We found Burl and Luca, Terry and Jen. A group of us settled around the white picnic table beside a birdbath.

"It's a tropical sickness," I told them.

"But we're not in the tropics," said Terry.

"Sharp observation," said Jen.

"Diseases are migrating fast these days," said Mattie. "Look at the bats. White-nose syndrome. And Lyme."

"Maybe the diagnosis is incorrect," said Luca.

"But Terry's mother's a doctor," I said.

"She's just a *gynecologist*," said Jen.

"Uh, yeah," said Terry. "An MD. Not a *cretin*."

"The good news is, dengue fever's not airborne," said Luca. "And it's a virus. So antibiotics aren't called for."

"You need to find out how bad it is," said Mattie. "Some of them may need transfusions."

"They'd be shit out of luck, then," said Jen.

"Not necessarily," said Burl. "There's decent medical equipment in the silo."

"I know how to transfuse," said Luca.

"I mean, do you have bags of *blood* in the silo too?" asked Terry, sarcastic.

"No," said Burl.

"*You'd* supply the blood," said Luca.

"No!" said Terry. "No no no no no."

"It would depend which parents need it, of course. But probably some of you would match your parents' types."

"We can't even get there," I said. "The bridge is out."

"We could walk the last mile," said Burl. "We could take the van. But just one vehicle. And no more gas. It could be dangerous."

"We don't even know if they need it," protested Jen. "I mean. Is dengue fever *serious*?"

I scrolled.

" 'Most patients recover in two to seven days,' " I read.

"See? No big deal," said Terry. He sat back, satisfied.

" 'However, some develop hemorrhagic fever, which can cause organ damage, bleeding under the skin, and death.' "

"Huh," said Terry.

"Can you find out who's sickest?" said Burl to me. "And how sick they are? If we go out there, it should only be to save lives."

"Everyone should text their parents," said Mattie. "Cast a wide net. Ask those two questions. See what you get."

We went around the yard and into the barn, finding the others and telling them. I waved down Low and Juicy, riding their ATVs around in mindless circles. They drove across the field toward me at high speed. Their tires churned up dirt and rocks, and they stopped fast at the last second. Dickheads. Made me jump.

"We have to message the parents," I said, and told them what they needed to do. That was when they reminded me their phones had been trashed in the storm. For the first time, they seemed happy about it. Even gleeful.

They wheeled their vehicles around and rode off again, whooping.

SUKEY SPENT ALL her time keeping the baby clean and fed and warm.

"Take a look," she said to Jen and me, a bit proudly. Her sister lay in the middle of the bed in a bundle of blankets.

The face was red and squashed, the top of the head a cone covered in black hair. She didn't move much.

"Hey, yeah!" I said. I wasn't sure what Sukey expected. I couldn't say the infant was adorable. I try not to lie. "Good job. You really stepped up," was what I decided on.

Then I looked at Sukey more closely. Her clothes were dirty, and her hair hung lank with grease.

"I know," I said. "I'll stay here with Jen. We'll watch the baby. You go take a break. Have a shower. OK?"

Jen helped me convince her, and then she was in the bathroom while we sat listening to the patter of the water.

On the bed the baby twitched in her sleep.

"People are out there with guns?" said Jen. "And we're supposed to drive through that to save *their* asses? *Them?*"

"Maybe," I said.

DEE'S MOTHER AND father were very sick. Also David's mother. And Low's (adoptive).

Adopted or not, though, Low knew his blood type: O negative. He was a universal donor.

He didn't want to go, not in the least.

But in the end he said yes.

BURL DISABLED THE fingerprint function temporarily and gave us the keys to the silo. "Go up to the top," he said as he climbed into the van. "Post a lookout. At all times. Text me if anything happens."

After they left, Dee and David and Low in the back of the van and Burl and Luca in front, Rafe and I climbed up.

At the top of the stairs, whose winding around the circular wall made me dizzy, was a landing with a door. We stepped out onto a metal platform that jutted out of the half-dome roof, with a rickety rail around it and a ratty plaid lawn chair.

I saw green fields broken by lines of trees, stretches of dirt road. The brown tops of scattered buildings, a farm to the right and a farm to the left. On the left side the backs of black-and-white cows, standing around an oblong tank, and on the right three kids in shorts, throwing a bright-yellow Frisbee.

"Are those the ones we're not supposed to hook up with?" asked Rafe.

"Rule number nine, I think."

As I watched them run and throw, the glide of the disk through the air, things felt normal for a second. I had a quick flash of suspicion: maybe we'd invented the rest. Made it up for a lark, the storm and falling-down trees. The dead mother.

I felt a quick pulse of relief. Until I realized I was inventing *this*. The real was fever. And ashes.

Far off was the blue of sky, blurring into a haze.

FOR A WHILE one of us was in the crow's nest whenever it was light. We kept Val's binoculars under the chair.

Val liked keeping watch, though she wasn't too vigilant. She tied a rope to the steel rail of the viewing platform and practiced climbing up and down. Rappelled faster and faster the more she practiced, grinning broadly when she kicked off against the silo's metal skin.

Rafe liked watch duty because he got to hit golf balls off the top with a club he'd stolen from the great house. Jen liked it because she got a break from helping with the baby. Terry liked it because he could write in his journal in privacy.

Not much happened up there. I looked at the sky as much as the road, stuck in my earbuds and listened to music. I let my mind dwell on our absent friends. Gone off to give their blood. Even Dee, compulsively sanitizing her hands and body, and David with his monkey-wrenching began to seem like saints.

Gone, they changed into abstractions. They were ideas, and ideas were more romantic than people.

I even daydreamed about Low once, in a reverie that arose from boredom. I shuddered as I did it. Embarrassed by my own daydreams. Recoiling, but also not as bored.

I wondered if a makeover would help. Usually it was women and girls that got makeovers, when in fact it was men and boys that needed them. If anyone did. I recalled various movies that featured makeover sequences, people becoming

the best-looking versions of themselves. Turning from cater-
pillars into butterflies. Montages set to inspiring music.

In movies, makeovers were treated like a triumph of the
human spirit.

It suggested we'd had a low bar for triumph, in recent
history. A dash of lipstick qualified, a haircut and some styl-
ing gel. A new outfit.

That was what the human spirit had turned into.

Meditations like those were the way *I* spent my time, on
top of the silo.

DAYS PASSED SLOWLY. It was a season of no storms and little
rain. By the calendar it wasn't fall yet, but somehow it wasn't
summer anymore either. Summer had been another time,
when we had a great house to go back to, a shining lake,
and the blue ocean.

In the mornings we took care of the donkeys and goats
and helped Mattie in the vegetable garden. We made lunch
in rotation. As afternoon wore on, we washed dirty clothes
in the cottage sink and hung them out to dry. We scrubbed
ourselves down with cold water, shared toothbrushes until
they fell apart, and used small dabs of toothpaste. Those of
us with periods had to cut a single sponge into pieces. We
boiled the pieces on the stove to sterilize them.

The angels refueled the generator with gas from the silo.
They liked to patrol the woods. We took turns cooking din-

ner with Darla and the angel named John, who'd been a sous-chef once. After dinner Sukey would take the baby to her mother's grave and give her a bottle and rock her to sleep. She was building a cairn at the grave with rocks from the stream, a couple more every day.

We mostly kept the lights off in the cottage, to save power and maintain a low profile. A few nights Rafe made fires outside, but we rationed them for safety. We'd gather close around the fire while the angels tried to teach us their hippie songs.

Darla said singing was good for your health.

"It's like smiling," she said. "The more you do it, the more you want to!"

Juicy spat.

They taught us a famous, sad song that went "Hello darkness my old friend, I've come to talk with you again," and a cheerful one called "Spirit in the Sky" that Jack liked because it talked about Jesus, his imaginary friend. The rest of us were OK with it because the angels said it was ironic. Written by a Jew from Massachusetts.

"Never been a sinner, I never sinned," we sang, off-key as the karaoke version played on our puck-shaped speaker. "I got a friend in *Jee*-sus."

Sometimes we yelled it, almost defiantly: *"Never been a sinner! I never sinned!"*

A PHOTO CAME by text, onto Rafe's phone from David's. A view of the library in the great house. Chairs and tables and sofas had been pushed to the sides of the room, against the tall bookshelves, and a row of mattresses had replaced them.

On the mattresses lay parents, and beside them David and Dee and Low. Zooming in, we could see thin red lines running between the arms of young and old. Graceful loops of tubing.

It reminded me of a news story I'd read, with photos, about a pharmaceutical lab. In it were hundreds of horse-shoe crabs whose blood was being harvested for medical testing. The machines siphoned off enough blood that the crabs didn't die but lived to be harvested again and again.

The company called it blood farming.

Beside me, Jack stared at the image as I zoomed. In the back, small and blurry, was the fireplace, and above it a painting of hunters with their hounds.

He touched the tip of his finger to the screen, moved it along a red loop of tube from David to David's mother. Tracing the swoops.

"He's going back where he came from," he said.

JACK AND SHEL were at a crucial moment in their "childhood journey," according to Darla. The time away from school and other kids their age could be "inhibiting their social and educational development."

She had an idea. "Our very own prairie school!" she cried, clapping her hands in delight. We cringed.

They could take classes: biology taught by Mattie, history taught by John, and poetry taught by her.

"The angels don't have enough to do," said Terry, when we conferred about it. "Could get antsy. Even destructive."

"Idle hands do the devil's work," said Rafe.

So we said yes. They could "teach" the little boys, if they wanted. We thanked them for their interest.

SOMETIMES I'D SIT in a parked car, motionless. I'd remember factories. I'd seen them onscreen in a hundred variations and always had the sense of them out there, churning, whirring, infinite moving pieces. Making the stuff we used.

Now I wondered if they were still busy, manufacturing. Or were shuttered and dark. Were other factories in other places doing the work they used to do? Or were certain components no longer made at all?

I let my eyes rest on a dashboard, its vinyl surfaces, the dust on the curves. I wondered what was behind the plastic and what parts of it were already obsolete.

My phone had ceased to interest me since the news started repeating, bringing a wash of grimness whenever I looked. I solved the problem by ignoring it.

The others abandoned theirs too—days would pass between updates. Rafe and David texted a check-in at night, just: *OK?* out. And *OK* back.

For a while that was it.

Before the storm we'd caught sight of the parents' screens sometimes, snagged their devices when we needed a quick fix. Gotten flashes of TV through a doorway. But these days we mostly had what was in front of us, the cottage and barn and long grass in the fields. Long and short, tussocks and bare patches. Topography. We had the wood of the walls and fences, the metal of the parked cars with their near-empty gas tanks.

We had the corners of buildings and the slope of the hills, the line of the treetops. The more time passed, the more any flat image began to seem odd and less than real. Uncanny delicate surfaces. Had we always had them?

We'd had so many pictures. Pictures just everywhere, every hour, minute, or second.

But now they were foreign. Now we saw everything in three dimensions.

POETRY CLASS TURNED out to be whatever Darla felt like saying. She also called it "humanities." Once she talked about a head lice incident in third grade.

"I was sent home *right in front* of the other kids," I heard her tell the little boys. "They *all knew*. They pointed at me. They go, *She's got lice! Cooties cooties cooties!*"

Another time she talked about a friend in Maine who raised alpacas for wool and made socks out of it. The socks were expensive, but darn they kept your feet warm in winter.

"And they're moisture-wicking," she told Jack.

Shel showed her the signs for *alpaca* and *sock*.

HISTORY WAS JOHN talking about places he'd visited—the Liberty Bell, Disneyland, the Museum of Ice Cream—but mostly it was the biography of his ex-girlfriend.

She'd broken up with him and he missed her.

BIOLOGY WAS THE best. It was held in the barn, where Mattie pulled up diagrams on his laptop and projected them onto a whitewashed wall.

Proterospongia, one was labeled. It looked like a tubular tree with eyeballs sprouting out of the ends of its branches.

"These," said Mattie, "are living examples of what the single-cell ancestor of *all* animals may have looked like."

Others joined the class, more every day. First there were just Jack and Shel. Then Juicy went, then Rafe, then Jen and Sukey, with the baby. Everyone. Some mornings they all went to sit in the barn. I'd watch from the open door and see them looking studious, their faces faithfully turned forward. They could have been children in school in a bygone era. In France when there were sun kings and halls of mirrors, in England before the world wars.

Children who sat there learning from their teachers, full of trust. Secure in the knowledge that an orderly future stretched ahead of them.

They sat quiet, gazing up at the projections.

Everything made by others, everything deliberate came rushing back to me. The rich colors and elegant lines. Illustrations, artists' renderings. There were cross sections and tree diagrams, diagrams like constellations and ladders and maps and spirals, and they told the story of the planet.

We saw the first appearance of liquid water, after the moon was formed. The earth three billion years ago, with tides a thousand feet high and hurricane-force winds. The time when oxygen entered the atmosphere, made by the algae that allowed for the rest of life. They showed when plate tectonics began. A timeline of the first sex.

Mattie said: "Sexual reproduction may have increased the rate of evolution."

People nodded, attentive. Even Juicy.

"First multicellular organism? Anyone? Eight hundred million years ago. Five hundred and fifty million years ago we find the first evidence of—? Good, Jack. Jellies, sponges, and corals. Five hundred thirty million years ago we find the first known footprints on dry land. It means that early animals may have explored the land before there were even *plants* growing there."

"How about the first animals with bones?" asked Jack.

"First vertebrates, four hundred eighty-five million."

The list of firsts went on so long it had to be continued from one day to the next. Each new form Mattie projected onto the barn's wall had its colors and details: here a nautilus, here a jawless fish, here the filaments of a fungus or small hairs called *cilia*.

He showed dinosaurs and ray-finned fishes, turtles, and flies. He showed silhouettes of trees with cones and told us they were gymnosperms. When they began to dominate the earth, he said, plant-eating animals had to grow to massive sizes to live off low-nutrition plants.

He showed a graph of extinction events, like the spiky line on a seismograph.

After a while we were so devoted to those pictures that we were almost disciples.

ONE EVENING AT dinner I ate half a piece of rye bread from a newly opened silo loaf before I noticed mold on it. Mattie looked closely at the mold, told the others not to eat it, and then tried not to panic while he looked for an emetic in the supply cabinet.

I took it, and he patted my back while I threw up into some bushes.

He said it had been toxic. It wouldn't kill me, now that I'd gotten rid of most of it, but the remnants in my system might give me hallucinations, like shrooms or peyote. Just drink a lot of water and sleep it off, he said.

I woke up confused in the middle of the night. Thought I heard a car outside.

Way out of it, head swimming and vision foggy, I climbed down the hayloft ladder with my legs shaking. The barn was dark except for a bulb in a cage that hung over the donkeys' stall. They stood close together, their heads lowered and facing the wall.

Someone was snoring, and I crept past wondering if I should be raising an alarm. But I was dizzy and couldn't think straight.

Pushing the barn door open with the flat of my hand, I saw Low and David beside the van. Its headlights were still on, and moths flitted around in the beams.

"Dee didn't come," said Low.

"She stayed with *them*," said David.

Their faces were in shadow, the van's beams behind them. I could only see hollows for eyes.

"She defected," said Low.

"Coward," said David.

"Traitor," said Low.

"Are the sick ones better?" I asked him.

"They're OK," said Low.

"Still dicks, though," said David.

"And what about Amy?"

"She was in the basement."

"What? That whole time?"

"Yeah. In a dark corner. Eating cereal from boxes."

The headlight shut off and the front doors of the van opened. Burl and Luca got out. David flicked on a flashlight. Duffels and sleeping bags were unloaded. I was relieved and not sure why—maybe because that was all.

Just the four of them. No parents had come along.

I felt a new rush of dizziness, looking at the ones who'd returned. Behind them, hazy, I thought I could see the absent parents when I squinted. The night blurred. Or maybe just the shapes of them, their effigies. Or no, it wasn't them, I realized—was it?

It was them and not them, maybe the ones they'd never been. I could almost see those others standing in the garden where the pea plants were, feet planted between the rows. They stood without moving, their faces glowing with some shine a long time gone. A time before I lived. Their arms hung at their sides.

They'd always been there, I thought blearily, and they'd always wanted to be more than they were. They should always be thought of as invalids, I saw. Each person, fully grown, was sick or sad, with problems attached to them like broken limbs. Each one had special needs.

If you could remember that, it made you less angry.

They'd been carried along on their hopes, held up by

the chance of a windfall. But instead of a windfall there was only time passing. And all they ever were was themselves.

Still they had wanted to be different. I would assume that from now on, I told myself, wandering back into the barn. What people wanted to be, but never could, traveled along beside them. Company.

7

No one went to poetry except the little boys, and even they only attended to protect Darla's feelings. She was always trying to take care of them.

I sat near them the morning after I hallucinated, dreamily folding laundry at the picnic table. Subdued. Recovering.

David and Low were throwing a tennis ball back and forth with the ones who'd stayed behind. They talked about the great house and the illness of the parents.

Darla must have been lecturing on pottery, because I caught the words *kneading the clay* and *indigenous*. Also *Mother Earth*.

Jack didn't have an active interest in ceramics. He cracked open his Bible, trying to peek inside unnoticed.

Her monologue trailed off.

"Is that your favorite book, dear?" she asked him.

"Fifth favorite. If you count series. I still like my old ones best. So it goes *Frog and Toad*, *George and Martha*, the *Guinness Book* and then *Laugh-Out-Loud Jokes*."

"What do you like about it?"

"Mostly that it's a mystery."

"The Bible is a mystery?"

"We solved a lot of it," said Jack. "The first clue was, God's code for nature. And then we figured out that trinity thing. With God and Jesus."

"What did you figure out, honey?"

Jack's eyes flitted over from Shel's signing hands.

"So if God stands for nature, then Jesus stands for science. That's why they call Jesus God's son. It doesn't mean *actual* son. God doesn't have *sperm*."

"Goodness! You know the birds and bees!"

"Darla. He's not in kindergarten," I said.

"It just means science comes from nature. See?"

He tipped his notebook so we could look.

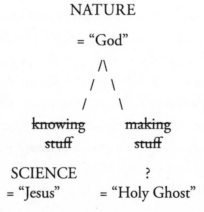

NATURE

= "God"

/\
/ \
/ \

~~knowing stuff~~   ~~making stuff~~

SCIENCE   ?
= "Jesus"   = "Holy Ghost"

A window crashed. I couldn't see which but heard glass break. Juicy ran by.

"Oh man. I broke it!" he yelled from around the corner of the cottage. "The bathroom window!"

"That looks *very* creative, sweetie," said Darla to Jack.

Juicy sauntered back and sat down heavily on the bench. Picking shards of glass out of the tennis ball.

"And the proof is, there's lots the same with Jesus and science," said Jack. "Like, for science to save us we have to believe in it. And same with Jesus. If you believe in Jesus he can save you."

"That makes, like, zero sense, small dude," said Juicy.

"It *does* make sense," Jack insisted.

"Ow!" said Juicy.

There was blood on his finger.

"See this, Juice? Science comes from nature. It's kind of a branch of it. Like Jesus is a branch of God. And if we believe science is true, then we can act. And we'll be saved."

Juicy stuck his bleeding finger in his mouth. "Saved like, go to heaven? Holmes, that's some Santa Claus *shit*."

"Your mouth is the least hygienic part of your body, Justin," said Darla.

She thought the name *Juicy* was undignified and called him by his given one, no matter how much he squirmed.

"No. Like the *earth*. The climate. The animals," said Jack. "Heaven's part of the code. It just means, a good place for us all to live."

"This stings a lot," said Juice.

"Why don't I get the peroxide," said Darla, and rose.

"Look," said Jack to Juicy, earnest. He turned a page in his notebook. "These are the miracles of Jesus, right? But they're all what science does too! *Almost* all. See? Proof."

Shel signed.

"Not a math proof, he says," said Jack. "It's not a math book. Just concepts."

Jesus = Science

		Jesus	Science
1.	Heals sick	✓	✓
2.	Makes blind people see	✓	✓
3.	Turns hardly any food into lots	✓	✓
4.	Walks on water (HOVERCRAFT!!)	✓	✓
5.	Raises the dead	✓	✗

4/5

"*Hovercraft?*" asked Juicy, peering.

"Shel really likes hovercrafts," said Jack. "They're an example, see? Of how science makes it so we can walk on water. Get it?"

Jack watched Shel sign and interpreted fast. I admired his fluency.

"Other examples are, science can freeze water. And when it's ice we can *walk* on it. Like Jesus did."

Darla came back carrying a box of Band-Aids.

"Also science can build bridges, and they go over water. There's like, a *lot* of things."

"That book was written like two thousand years ago," said Juicy. "Science wasn't even *invented* then."

"You're very ignorant," said Shel. Out loud.

"Sheldon!" said Darla, after a moment. Face wreathed in smiles. "You can *talk*!"

I'd never heard him speak before either. I'd known he could—Jack and Jen had both told me. But he spoke only on special occasions.

Juicy's ignorance qualified, I guess.

"Sure he can," said Jack, shrugging.

"What a wonderful self-expression, honey," said Darla to Shel. "Humanities is over, boys."

THE STORMS BEGAN again. Up and down the coast they came rolling in.

The barn was built on higher ground than the great house, and the trees were mostly set apart, across the field. Too far from our buildings to crash through the barn or cottage roof. By the time they made it inland, the storms were tamer.

Still, it rained constantly. We played games on makeshift

boards we drew with chalk on the barn's cement floor, but when we argued about rules the games broke down. Energy dissipated.

Jen kept Terry on a short leash, sometimes ignoring him, then making out with him when she had nothing better to do. I didn't make out with Low. No matter how many times he tried to brush up against me accidentally, I couldn't muster an interest. It was less the tie-dyed shirts and sandals themselves (plus old banana) than the way he didn't notice how we looked at them.

A lack of self-awareness, that was Low's problem.

We sat around and listened to the angels tell stories. Mistakes they'd made, their lives' worst situations. And strangest. The time on a fishing ship in Alaska when Luca's job was to cut the heads off flatfish the size of sofas. The time he saw an eyeball dangling out of a woman's eye socket after an accident and had to tape a paper cup over it. The time on a raft in Norway when he watched the blue ice of towering glaciers fall into the warming sea, and a man sat at a piano on an ice floe.

The glacier fell like water, he said, and the man played a funeral song.

At one of his jobs, Mattie'd got half a finger in the mail from a man who went to jail. Another time he walked barefoot on the sands of a Brazilian island at night and stepped onto the broken neck of a beer bottle. It went all the way through the top of his foot.

"See? Entry and exit wounds," he said, and pulled off a sandal to show us the scars.

We liked the angels. They hadn't brought us into the world—they hadn't brought anyone into it—and in that fact we felt a bond. In that fact we were equals.

I GOT INTO the habit of walking around the farm by myself when the rain was light. I'd find a quiet place and just stand there, listening to the patter of drops on the leaves and ground. I closed my eyes to see what else I could hear.

I practiced forgetting what was beyond me and noticing only where I was. I practiced being wet and cold and hungry and not minding.

Sometimes I took Jack with me, along with a field guide from the closet that we consulted through plastic. We learned the names of the trees and bushes and looked up their histories. We learned which had grown here in the time of the Indians and which had been brought from far away. Maples from Norway, mulberries from Asia, Siberian elm.

A tree from China called the empress.

EVENTUALLY WE GAVE up our custom of keeping watch. Socked in the way we were, enclosed by low clouds, we had no visibility from the silo.

Also we feared lightning. So we stopped going up.

It was the rain that kept us off the watchtower, so it was the rain that brought the men with guns.

WE WERE SITTING around the table in the cottage kitchen when a man we'd never seen before walked right in.

He slid a gun from his coat. We got up quickly.

He smelled bad, not like sweat but something else—gas, maybe. (Motor oil and raw meat, Rafe said later.) He had gray hair in a crew cut and a bushy beard, like all men suddenly. He was wearing filthy jeans and a camo vest over a bright T-shirt, the orange of pylons. There was an edge of energy to him like a sick buzz.

He showed the gun to us, matter-of-fact. It looked heavy. He said, "How'd you end up sitting around here, kids? All fat and happy?"

We stared at him. We weren't fat.

And we didn't feel too happy, either.

He said, "What's your secret?"

He didn't say it nicely.

Gesturing with his gun, he made us file out the door. Then he talked on a walkie-talkie and marched Luca down to open the locked gate.

We could see trucks and Jeeps waiting.

I ran to the barn to find the little boys. "Jack," I whispered. "There are guys with guns here. You and Shel need to grab some camping gear and run. Into the woods. Stay hidden till I come looking for you."

"I don't want to leave you, Evie," said Jack.

"I need you to, you see? I mean it. Go! Go! Go now!"

Once they were gone, dropping down from the hay door in the back, I went outside again. The motorcade was coming through the gate. More men sat in the backs of the trucks. They looked like soldiers, minus the neatness and uniforms.

"Redneck soldiers," said Rafe.

Some were standing on the running boards of a Jeep, outside the doors, holding onto a rack on the top. Their guns were chunky and long. The men parked the cars messily, and one truck ran over the fence around the vegetable garden. Ripped the wire out of the ground and rolled right over our best tomato plants.

When I saw that, my face felt hot.

Luca said we could offer them sandwiches, but then they should go. There was a baby here, he said. An infant. And youth. "Recovering from trauma."

A soldier punched him hard in the shoulder, while the others got busy rummaging.

We stood outside the cottage and waited. One of them was around our age, a redhead with prominent acne. He guarded the door with his gun while cabinet doors slammed and pots crashed and banged.

The men came out stuffing food in their mouths, and when I peeked around into the empty kitchen I saw the contents of drawers and cabinets spilled all over the floor. The aftermath of a burglary.

IT WASN'T LONG before they found the silo. They rounded us up and herded us into the barn, and there the leader gave a short speech.

"You're gonna let us in," he said.

What was locked up had value, and what had value was food. Therefore. For every five minutes that we didn't let them in, a penalty would happen.

We looked around at each other, knowing Burl was the key. I couldn't see him.

"You," said the leader to Mattie, who had a protective arm around Sukey. The baby was making squawks, and Sukey was bouncing her to keep her from wailing full-out.

"Yes?" said Mattie.

"Move. Over there. Put your hand on the bench."

It was the tool bench, along the wall Mattie used for his projections. The barn door was open, and I saw one long, single-strand cobweb float off the side of the bench in the light from outside, snagged on a splinter.

I remember that cobweb.

So Mattie stood beside the bench. Rested his hand on it. One of the soldiers took a rope and tied the hand to the vise on the bench's end. The leader held a power tool, yellow and black. I stared at it.

"Staple gun," whispered Rafe.

The leader turned and switched it on. It made a grating noise, and I saw Mattie flinch.

"In five minutes I put a staple through that hand," said the leader.

Angels were looking at each other, faces strained. Where was Burl? Not there. I glanced around. I didn't want to rat him out, and I sure didn't want the soldiers to take our food.

But then there was the staple gun.

"The lock is biometric," said someone.

Darla. I wasn't surprised she was the first to cave.

"Say what?"

"You need a fingerprint to open it."

"Whose?" said the leader.

"He's not in here," said Luca.

"That's too bad," said the leader, and before I knew it he turned and Mattie cried out. Blood ran down his hand from a staple right through the center of his palm.

He stopped yelling and looked like he was trying not to cry, his lips tight. He pushed air out of his mouth in quick huffs and said, "OK. OK. OK."

"I'll go find him," said Luca.

"I'll help," I said, because I had to get out of there.

Outside the barn it was way easier to breathe.

We ran instead of walked, calling for Burl as we went. When we found him, behind the cottage messing with the generator and listening to music on some borrowed earbuds, he was clueless.

We told him the deal and went back into the barn.

Mattie called, "Burl! Don't let them take the food!"

The leader punched another staple into his hand.

THEY HUSTLED BURL out the barn door and left Mattie stapled, guarded by the redheaded kid. At the back of the crowd Rafe grabbed my sleeve, a finger to his lips. We hovered there till the men were all outside.

The kid wore his red hair straggly at the back, a mullet. He had a classic chipped tooth, right up front. His tan work boots hung off his ankles unlaced, tongues lapping out and laces dragging, and his white tank top was finger-smeared black across the stomach.

He chose that moment to break his long gun open. Sat down on a hay bale with it braced on his skinny knee, shoving in a shell.

"Grab it," whispered Jen, and elbowed Rafe. "He can't shoot while he's loading!"

"But what if he closes it in time?" asked Rafe.

"Now! Now!" said Jen, and we both elbowed him.

Awkwardly he walked up to the kid and grabbed the open gun. They wrestled for a minute—Mattie was watching from the tool bench, blood pooling around his tied-down hand—until Rafe kneed the kid in the balls. He grunted and dropped the weapon.

A shell rolled on the floor.

"Here!" said Jen, and jumped on the gun before the kid could straighten up.

"Hide it," Rafe told her. "Just hide it somewhere."

I went to Mattie, peered at the staples. They were sunk in deep. I could barely see them, just puffy skin and blood.

"We're going to need Luca," he said. His forehead was sweating, and it was hard for him to talk. "Will you get Luca? Maybe he can take them out."

Sounds of crashing glass in the distance, muffled. We ran out to see. There was a crowd at the base of the silo, and from the back I couldn't see much. Then soldiers streamed out, cheering and shaking the guns they held.

"Lookit this! H&K MP5!"

"I got a Ruger!"

"I got a vintage six-shooter!"

"Vintage is crap."

The leader came out after them with Burl walking behind him, his hands attached to each other at the wrists. The plastic ties I'd seen police use on TV shows.

"Come on," said Burl. "Cut off the flex cuffs. What am I going to do? I'm a little outgunned here, don't you think?"

"You want me to believe you got nothing but peanut butter and peaches left? You think I'm buying that?"

"And all that rice!" said Burl. "We'll miss the bags of rice. Leave us just one, will you? One bag."

The angels were clustered around. Jen tugged on Luca's sleeve, asking him to help Mattie, and the soldiers sat on the hoods of trucks and on the ground loading up their new guns, breaking open boxes of bullets they'd stolen.

"One bag!" chanted Darla. "One bag! One bag!"

Her numerous bracelets jangled as she clapped. It irritated me.

"Shh," David urged her.

"What's that?" said the leader suddenly. He pointed.

We followed his gaze. On the edge of the meadow near the woods, three of the goats could be seen.

"Sheep tastes bad," said a man with a crossbow.

"*Lamb's* tasty," said the leader.

"That's not lamb. That there's a full-grown sheep."

"They're goats, in fact," said Terry.

"Goat *really* tastes like shit," said the leader.

"Solid protein, though," said the crossbow.

There was a shot. I almost screamed. A goat buckled and fell. The other two took off.

I turned around and around, my breath stopped, till I pegged where the shot had come from: the redhead, shooting from the door in the hayloft. He had a small gun this time. He raised his arms in the air and yelled. *Whoo-hoo.*

Jack was out there. Jack was behind the goats.

"Jack could be hit!" I hissed, low, to Burl. "*Jack's* over there!"

"Stop him from shooting," said Burl to the leader. "Come on, man."

The kid raised his handgun again. My body got tense. I looked back at the fallen goat, a white lump on the ground, and saw what I feared most.

Jack ran out from under the trees and dropped to his knees beside the goat.

"Oh no oh no oh no," I think I said. I looked back and forth frantically between him and the gun kid, who wasn't noticing. Just celebrating his shot. Waving his weapon in the air, dancing around in the hayloft door.

"Is he . . . ?" said David.

"Seems like a full retard," nodded Juicy.

Luckily the leader—the other men called him *governor*—had walked off toward his muddy truck, and as the kid raised his gun again he passed him, yelling something. The kid looked bummed out, but relaxed his arm.

I took off across the field to Jack.

He was on his knees crying over the goat, who was breathing weakly and bleeding from a hole in her rib cage.

"Dilly, Dilly," sobbed Jack. The goats had tags on their collars with names on them. "She's the only LaMancha goat here. She's so sweet. She's the sweetest goat ever."

I wanted to stay with him, but I knew I couldn't.

So when the goat stopped breathing I led him back into the woods, where Shel was hunkered down behind a clump of thick undergrowth.

I never raised my voice to Jack, but that time I came close.

MATTIE HAD BEEN freed when I made it back to the barn. Pale, he lay on his back across some bales while Luca wrapped gauze around his hand.

"Nice place you got," said the governor to Burl, and then his men took over the cottage.

He posted guards at the kitchen door, the two fattest soldiers. They wore plaid shirts and carried rifles over their shoulders on slings.

"Why aren't they leaving?" I asked Burl.

"They don't believe that's all our food. They figure they're going to starve the rest out of us. And eat the goat."

"We should have gotten the guns out before," I said. "Then they wouldn't *have* all of them."

I knew it was wrong before it was out of my mouth.

"Eve. Please," said Burl, even more wearily than usual. Disappointed in me, I could see. I didn't like the feeling. "If we'd gotten the guns out, we'd be dead."

THEY HADN'T NOTICED the vegetables in the garden, so I got Jen and we dug together. We carried carrots and kale in our shirts, several loads, and hid the pile inside a rotting log.

Then we saw Mattie being led out of the barn. He was still a hostage, I guess. Or a scapegoat. The two fat guards tied him to a tree, a delicate tree that grew beside the cottage. He gazed into the branches as they tightened the knots.

The soldiers dragged Dilly's body into the middle of the yard. They leaned over, their ass cracks fully exposed, and butchered it. A fat guard pulled out what looked like long gray sausages. Intestines, maybe.

Jen threw up.

"Ha ha ha ha," said the red-haired kid.

I wanted to stab him.

IN THE DARK of the hayloft we lay in our row of sleeping bags whispering, some of us trying to plot a rebellion. But soon the whispers stopped. As long as the soldiers held their weapons, and their weapons were loaded, rebellion wasn't getting much traction.

I slipped out of my bag and climbed down the ladder. Couldn't find my shoes, but I wasn't planning to go far. So I went out the barn door barefoot and trekked over the grass to where Burl and the angels slept in their tents.

I was just raising my hand to slap at his door flap when I heard him speaking, low.

"They're killing the rest of the goats tomorrow," he said.

"Then what?" asked someone. Luca, probably.

"You," said a voice behind me.

Something metal poked into my back and I tried to turn, but it jabbed me.

I knew who it was: the redhead.

"Come on," he urged. "I'll shoot your foot."

Full retard, Juicy had said. I didn't know about that, but I was afraid of him: he seemed like a guy who couldn't predict his own actions.

So I shuffled away from Burl's tent, wondering if I should yell. The kid's gun scraped against my backbone.

"I seen you go out in the trees," he said. "You're *hiding* something."

"I go out there to pee, that's all," I said. I did pee in the forest, it was true. We all did. We had a rule: the cottage toilet was exclusively for number two.

"You're hiding food. You have a stash. And now you're showing me."

"Now? In the dark? There's nothing *there*," I protested. I didn't want him to find Jack.

"Someone outside?" came Burl's voice.

"Don't say anything," said the redhead. "Go on. Move!"

"Can I get my shoes?"

"Move!"

I picked my way across the field barefoot, the kid poking me with his gun constantly. My vision adjusted as the trees drew up in front of us, a black mass filling the sky.

I didn't know where to lead him. Jack and Shel were out there, and here I was in the dark with a trigger-happy moron who thought I could lead him to the end of the rainbow.

Still, Mattie was worse off than I was by far. *He* wasn't complaining.

"There isn't anything out here but trees and bushes," I said as I stepped carefully. "There's nothing to see."

He snapped a light on. A blazing white glare to either side of us, and then ahead of us when he took the gun out of my back. He passed me on the trail between tree trunks.

"You run, I'm gonna shoot you," he told me.

"You mentioned that," I said.

I stepped on a sharp branch with a bare foot and gasped, and the kid spooked and whirled on me. I held up my arms, like that would help.

"It hurt," I said. My foot throbbed, and I limped.

His light hypnotized me as we wound through the trees. I stared at the leaves and branches it lit up in front of us, trying to think of a strategy for avoiding the little boys. Where were we even going? But nothing came to me. My mind was blank. Maybe we'd walk forever. Maybe we'd walk sheer out of the woods again and into a nothingness beyond.

Maybe I didn't care anymore.

There was a pattern to the sticks on the ground ahead of him, I noticed while he whistled some irritating tune. The pattern reminded me of pies we used to eat at Thanksgiving, each with a lattice of crust on top. What kind of pies had they been? Apple? Blueberry?

I would love a pie right now, I thought.

He stumbled and his light jerked. He was falling.

Leaves and branches snapped and crackled, and I heard squeals. The white light angled up from below.

He'd stepped through the mesh into a hole deeper than he was tall.

From down in the hole, he screamed and shouted as I peered in.

"My leg! I broke my leg! Help me!"

But he still had his gun, so I left.

It was probably a trapping pit, Burl told me when I got back. The woods weren't on the owner's land. Some people hunted and trapped there.

Any of us could have broken a leg, I wanted to whine. Or even a neck. But I was grateful for the pit. And then I went to sleep.

We were groggy when the soldiers burst into the barn. It took me a minute to understand they were angry. We all sat up rubbing our eyes and blinking as they crashed the butts of their guns into posts and hanging lightbulbs.

It was morning.

"The goats! Where the fuck are the goats?" shouted one.

The goats had made themselves scarce, apparently.

"Fucking OK," said the governor. "You fucking kids. You're gonna pay."

And they turned around and stamped out again. In confusion the rest of us followed, stuffing our feet into our shoes, climbing out of our stalls and down from the hayloft.

Beneath the tree Mattie was standing again, his arms strung up in the branches. Some of the men were aiming their guns at him.

"Why do you think they ran off?" shouted Burl. "Gunshots! That was you!"

"Get over here," said the fat guards, and poked at the angels with their rifles until all three of them were inside the circle of razor wire stretched around Mattie and his tree.

Only Burl was left outside the circle—Burl and us.

And the soldiers.

"Go find the goats," said the governor, in our direction. "For each five minutes we don't see some goats, I'm going to go like this," and he stuck what looked like a big, long red fork past the razor wire.

It touched Darla's side and she jumped, screaming.

"Cattle prod," muttered Terry.

The governor poked again and again, till she fell on the ground and writhed and scratched herself on a razor blade. Blood dripped down her forehead.

"Find 'em," said the governor.

"Head wounds just bleed a lot," Burl told us. "She'll be OK. Do what he says, I guess."

JACK AND SHEL had herded the goats through the shallowest part of the creek. Past the caved-in trapping pit, where the redhead was sleeping, cradling his shotgun. Through the trees, along a gravel road past a broken-down garage and the rusted teeth of a plow. Past a peeling billboard for satellite TV. Into a fenced pasture next to a neighbor's house—one of the houses you could see from the silo.

There were black-and-white cows standing around, and the goats browsed on some long grass at the far side.

"If we bring them back they're going to shoot them," said Jack. "Like he shot Dilly. Like *Dilly*."

"But if we don't, they'll hurt the angels more," said Rafe.

"Or one of us," I said.

"It's not fair. Why should *they* have to die?" asked Jack, starting to cry.

"Jack, look at me," I said. "We have to take them back. It's serious."

"It's not their *fault*," cried Jack. "We're not supposed to sacrifice the animals. We're supposed to *save* them. I'd rather sacrifice *me*."

"But the soldiers don't *want* you," I said. "They don't eat little boys, you see."

"They don't eat us," mumbled Jack.

Eventually the small boys headed toward the far side of the pasture. We waited by the farmhouse, whose front porch had some skateboards on it and a jumble of scooters and muddy boots. I knocked on the door, but no one was home.

Through the windows we could see the living room with daylight streaming in. It was full of toys, sitting in rows on the carpet like a kindergarten class. In front of them, in an armchair, sat a giant plush lion, the kind you win playing games at fairs. It had an open picture book on its lap.

I expected the lion to turn the page.

Then I heard a *baa* and saw the goats picking their way toward us, Jack and Shel trudging in front of them.

We made our way back down the road.

Jack and Shel sniffed miserably, petting the goats now and then on their backs and heads. The rest of us were distracted and anxious. I was thinking of the razor wire, and Mattie's hand that had looked dark and shot through with black veins.

But the goats' death sentence hung over me too. I glanced

sidelong at their faces as we led them into the trees again, their sleepy eyes with long white lashes. Their wet noses and blunt little horns, their gently sloping backs.

When Jack rested his hand on their fur they seemed no different from our dogs, back at the great house.

Contented. Wagging their stubby tails.

SOLDIERS HAD BEEN sticking angels with the cattle prod and watching them thrash. Thrashing, their legs and arms got sliced up on the razors.

But by the time we got back, leaving the goats in the field and Jack and Shel in the woods, they'd stopped. Sukey had come outside with the baby, said Burl. She'd stood there bouncing the infant and staring at the soldiers. Until finally they gave up. The baby was a buzzkill, I guess.

Now two of them were peeing against the cottage wall while another one played a game on his phone. When they noticed the goats they checked that their guns were loaded and went off.

The angels were crumpled on the ground inside the razor wire, arms and ankles bloody. Above them Mattie sagged against the thin trunk of the dogwood. His knees were bent, and he was hanging from his tied-up wrists. It looked like he was sleeping.

We held the wire down so Low and Rafe could step over it. They lifted Luca first. His feet dragged across the ground as they carried him between them over the clumpy grass. In the barn we laid him on some hay bales and went back for John and Darla.

I asked Burl if we could untie Mattie and take him too, but Burl shook his head.

We shouldn't go that far. Might tip the scales, he said.

Behind us the governor stood up high in the hayloft door, lord of all he surveyed. He scoped around with one hand stuck in his button-down shirt, like a painting of Napoleon.

DARLA HAD THE worst injuries. Patches of blood on her hippie tunic made its yellow sleeves red. In barely a whisper from his bank of bales, Luca said two of her cuts needed stitches: one was gaping open and still bleeding. Juicy offered to sew it up—he was getting into gore lately—but Burl said no thanks, he'd handle it.

So Luca walked him through stitching Darla's cuts, and we sat beside them. She was passed out at first, but then she woke up and moaned. Luca heaved himself over to us shakily and gave her a shot of painkiller from the medical kit, and Burl wiped a cotton ball with iodine around the biggest cut.

She got giggly and started talking nonsense and slurring her words. "Razor blades," she giggled. "Razor, eraser, razor eraser razor raze! Raisin!"

But she let Burl stick the needle back in.

It was while we were watching the needle poke in and

out of the flaps of skin—Low fascinated, Jen throwing up in the corner—that we heard the shots.

I stuck my fingers in my ears. I knew it looked childish, but I thought of the wagging tails and sleepy eyes and couldn't help it.

"Why are they shooting them all at once?" asked Juicy. "Won't the meat go rotten if they don't eat it right away?"

"They have a big freezer," said Burl. "A walk-in. Didn't you hear? They're living in a McDonald's."

THE SOLDIERS BRAGGED about the stainless countertops and taps in the sinks that still ran water so hot it could scald you. The heavy bags of frozen French fries in the walk-in freezer. They'd cut up the carcasses there, in the comfort of their industrial kitchen.

Carrying the goats by the legs, they swung them up into the beds of two pickups. Hooves and horns clanged on the metal.

Jack was deep in the forest, his face turned away. Had to be, right? I asked Jen. He was *not* seeing this.

Neither was Shel, she said. We looked hard at each other. Like if we looked hard enough, we could make it true.

But the governor still wasn't convinced we'd given up all the food. When the goat killers drove off he kept six men with him, including the two fat guards and the guy who carried a crossbow. And he left Mattie tied to the tree. He took his soldiers into the silo and ferried loads of supplies into their Jeeps.

We hung out in the barn, the three bandaged angels lying down, the rest of us sitting on bales.

"You're not taking me seriously," the governor said to Burl, standing at the door when the loading had tapered off. "You think I'm joking."

"I do not," said Burl.

"We know you're *not* joking," said Darla. She was still loopy from the painkiller Luca had given her. Lay on her back twirling her greasy dreads around a finger, arms wrapped in white bandages. She'd moved her jangly bracelets to her ankles. I knew them well by then: fish charms and peace signs, crescent moons and stars, spirals and yin-yang symbols. "But you've got a *very black* aura."

"Zip it, Darla," said Rafe.

"I'm gonna shoot that guy," said the governor. "The teacher."

"He's a biologist," said Sukey.

She was holding the baby laid across her lap in its blanket, where it looked like an oversized cocoon.

"I don't care if he's Tarzan King of the Apes. If I don't hear where the rest of your food is by sundown, I'm gonna shoot him in the gut," said the governor. "Slow and painful. Sunset. Don't say I didn't warn you."

"You have huge bags of frozen fries," said Juicy. "Your guys said so."

"Plus we can't give you what we don't have," said Burl.

I thought they had balls, talking to him like that.

"None of your fucking business what I have. Sunset," said the governor.

He kicked the leg of a donkey as he went out.

It shied, then flicked its tail.

Juice gathered some spit, but turned his face away from us to expel it. He'd gotten more mature.

"One hundred percent douche," he said.

THE RAIN HAD let up after the soldiers arrived, but now it started to fall again. We went out to Mattie's tree and stretched the fly of his tent above him, trying to keep him dry, but he was already soaked. Still he smiled faintly as Val and I propped a dry sleeping bag around his wet shoulders.

"When they find that kid who fell into the pit, he's going to tell on me," I said to Burl, as we stepped back into the barn. "You think I'll get punished?"

He got out some fresh cotton batting and started peeling off the bandages around one of Darla's arms. Rafe and Jen sat down near her head and put their hands on her shoulders to keep her from jerking.

"I don't think they care about that kid," he said, as he pulled away some soaked cotton.

"Kid's a half-wit," said Terry.

"I think he just tagged along," said Burl.

"Oh oh oh oh," said Darla.

"The drug's worn off," said Rafe.

"It hurts," said Darla.

Then Luca was standing up from his bales. He swayed.

"I'll do it," he said, and took the cotton from Burl.

Crickets began to chirp, from different parts of the barn at the same time.

There shouldn't have been crickets.

"The phones," said Juicy. "It's phones."

And it was. Some of them still had a charge, and the ringers defaulted to crickets. They were all ringing at once.

8

M Y PHONE WASN'T one of those phones, because I'd long
since abandoned it in a kitchen drawer. So I wasn't
one of the ones who answered. I wasn't one of the ones that
brought them.

I don't say it to claim I'm innocent, I just say it because
it's true.

There's that common expression that goes: Don't bring
a knife to a gunfight.

But a knife is better than nothing.

AT ONE HOUR till sunset we stood in the rain on the top
of the silo, shivering and watching Mattie droop from his
wrists whenever he passed out. I could see him through the

bare branches above his head: most of the leaves had been stripped off them.

The soldiers liked to slash at the tree with their rifles, right above Mattie's head.

He would jerk awake when the weight on his wrists hurt too much, then drop as he passed out again. I kept thinking about how we would finally get him untied. How his arms would fall to his sides, the best relief there could be. Then we'd carry him off to safety. We'd wash him and take care of his hands and give him clean clothes to wear.

We'd let him rest in a soft place.

I glanced down at Burl, standing beneath me on the landing of the spiral stairs. I looked at his narrow shoulders and lined face. I thought how weary he looked.

He'd let us in through the biometric door and we'd all climbed to the top. The governor and his soldiers didn't try to stop us—they'd already taken all that the silo offered. We'd heard their laughing and music from the cottage as we dashed through the rain. The cottage windows were all lit up and cast a yellow light on Mattie's tree.

We waited up in the crow's nest, tense. All of us except Sukey, who was down at the bottom with the baby, and the angels, lying in the barn nursing their wounds. We crowded each other so much on the platform I was afraid someone would fall off.

Then familiar cars were coming up from the gate, their tires crunching on gravel. Three of them, three cars we knew. One of them was my parents'.

There was always debris on the floor of our car. Empty chip bags and crushed seltzer cans and flecks of white-cheddar popcorn. It used to annoy me every time I stepped on it. Now I felt almost fond, remembering that trash. The remains of plentiful snacks.

It hadn't occurred to me to pick it up. I always waited for my parents to take care of it.

Once we had let them do everything for us—assumed they would. Then came the day we didn't want them to.

Still later we found out that they hadn't done everything at all. They'd left out the important part.

And it was known as: the future.

"What did you tell them?" I asked David.

"We said the soldiers had rifles."

"Maybe they've got something we don't know about," said Juicy, hopeful. "A secret weapon."

We mulled it over. I had a drifting feeling as we watched the parents get out of their cars, saw the doors slam behind them. Drifting or floating.

I was high above the action and I wished I could stay there. Forever. Up in the silo or even flying. I could glide over everything, the farm and the fields, watching what happened below but never needing to act.

I could stay up in the air for all time, as long as Jack was floating beside me.

"Who are we kidding," said Rafe.

EIGHT PARENTS HAD come, including mine. Newly thin. Chaos had slimmed them down. Like a movie star's personal trainer.

But if they had secret weapons, those weapons were well hidden.

We watched them walk over to Mattie's tree and stop, standing around it in the drizzle.

They didn't know anything about him, I thought. They had no idea how good he was.

I wished I could see their faces. Darkness was gathering.

Sunset, the governor had said. We were anxious.

We thought we should go out, then wondered if our presence would distract them. I was heading down the stairs when Burl called up from below.

"Stay put," he said. "You're liabilities. I'll tell them what the deal is."

He should hurry, I thought. Before the soldiers surprised them, or they surprised the soldiers.

"Get out there then," said Juicy. He had no problem being rude.

"It's going to be sunset soon," said Rafe, apologetic.

"I'm going now," said Burl.

"I want to come with you," said Val.

"Are *your* parents out there?"

"Not out there. No parents."

They walked out the silo door, and the rest of us stayed in the crow's nest.

We saw Burl talking to the parents at the tree, and one split off—a father, but not mine. Mine was kneeling beside my mother. Apparently, tying the laces on her shoe.

Sometimes she had back pain, so he'd do her bending-down for her. Her back must be hurting, now.

He wasn't all bad, my father.

The other father jogged to his car and came back carrying a kit. He took something out and clipped the razor wire. It fell, and they untied Mattie.

Juicy tried to high-five Rafe, but Rafe was too cool for high-fiving. Burl led a couple of fathers toward the barn— they were carrying Mattie, his arms around their shoulders and his head lolling back.

The loud music from the cottage stopped. A whining country-type voice was cut off in mid-note.

We peered over, craning our necks, squeezed tight beside each other at the rail. The governor came out the door and behind him the two fat guards, unslinging their weapons. There was talk, raised voices, but we couldn't make out the words.

Then someone pushed someone. We weren't clear who. There were too many people standing close. A gun went off. Two screams. We stared at each other's faces.

But it looked like the shot had been into the air, because no one staggered. The parents fell back.

There were guns held to fathers' backs. Mothers were saying panicky things in high voices. The last soldiers came out of the cottage. Their weapons were gesturing—even the crossbow, jerking toward the barn. The group was walking.

"*Should* we go down?" asked Jen.

"We're wusses if we stay here," said Juice.

"Burl *told* us to," said Low.

"Respect to Burl," said Rafe. "Remember? It's a rule."

"You stay right here," called up Sukey.

"Look what I found!" called a second voice. Also from downstairs.

I ducked inside and looked. Val stood at the silo door. She beckoned behind her.

It took me a second to recognize Dee. Was she thinner, like the parents? Had they run out of food at the house? Or was it just that her face seemed old?

"Well, looky there," said Low.

"She was hiding in a car," said Val.

"They needed help getting here," said Dee weakly. "And it was *you* who wanted them. *You* said you needed their help."

"Only because they called us," said Low.

"You called them *first*," said Dee.

"Did *not*," said Low, indignant.

"Well, someone did," said Dee. "That's how they knew where you were. And why they all called you. At the same time."

"Bull," said Rafe. "None of us called them."

We shook heads.

"Did not call," said Jen.

"Nope," said Low. "We wouldn't *ever*."

"*I* called."

We looked down. Sukey, bouncing the baby. She didn't even raise her face. She didn't meet our gaze.

We were silent.

I could barely believe it.

But she'd said it. She'd said it herself.

"So yeah," said Dee. "I'm right. I win."

"You don't win shit," said Jen.

But she looked defeated. She'd been closer to Sukey than any of us.

"Fan-fucking-tastic," said Rafe, after a minute. "Useless. And now those psychos have eight new hostages."

"What's our next move?" asked Juicy.

He looked to Rafe, and Rafe looked to me.

I thought of Jack and Shel, hiding out undetected. Part of me still wanted us to take off and join them. Leave the elders to fight it out.

But I couldn't.

So we talked. And we voted.

THE DELEGATION WAS me and Rafe and Terry. Sukey and Dee tagged along—Dee insisted on it, and Sukey had the baby. David stayed in the silo.

The rest rappelled down on Val's climbing rope and set out for the woods in the dark. Our group crossed to the barn, where the guy with the crossbow was guarding the door.

Inside it was dim, a few camp lanterns hanging from

beams. The parents were stuck in a stall, with the door pad-
locked. I wasn't sure what the padlock was for, since the stall
had a half-wall. They could have climbed out. But whatever.

In another stall were Burl and the angels, bent over taking care of Mattie.

The soldiers seemed to have forgotten him. Or maybe
they'd finally taken pity.

I doubted it.

"Eve!" said my mother.

"Eve!" said my father.

There was a strange aspect to them, beyond their gaunt
frames and faces. It hit me: they were stone-cold sober.

"Aw. Family *reunion*," jeered the crossbow guy.

"Oh my God," said my mother. "You're OK. And Jack.
Where's Jack?"

"He's safe," I said. "For now."

"Eve. We were *so* worried."

"We told you they had guns," I hissed. "And you came
here with absolutely nothing?"

"We have the law on our side, Eve," said my father, drawing himself up straight, his eyes meant to be blazing. "The
power of the law!"

Maybe he *was* drunk, after all.

"We threatened litigation," said a father next to him.

The father must have been Rafe's, because Rafe buried
his face in one hand and shook his head.

"We're going to sue the pants off these bastards," muttered another father. "When things get back to normal."

"A baby! The *baby*!" crooned a mother, and the mothers clustered at the stall door, trying to touch her. Sukey held up the baby and let them.

We turned away from the baby-petting.

TERRY WAS OUR spokesperson, as usual, though without his glasses he looked less scholarly. A dumpy little guy, Terry.

"Excuse me. Where's the governor?" he asked the crossbow man.

The crossbow pointed.

The other soldiers were up in the hayloft, sitting on bales and our piled-up bedding. Smoking. The smell of pot wafted.

I didn't like their greasy asses on my sleeping bag. Not one bit.

"Sir," called Terry. "May we have your attention?"

"Sure, kid," said the governor, and took a joint from one of the fatties. "Nothing better to do."

They'd given up on the sunset deadline, anyway. The parents had distracted them, at least.

"In private," said Terry.

"Come on up," said the governor, inhaling deeply. And holding it in.

So we climbed the ladder, first Terry, then Rafe, then me.

"You gonna tell us where the rest of the stash is?" said the governor. "Or do we have to torture those parents?"

Beside him a fatty brandished a small black thing that looked like my father's shaving clippers.

"Taser. Delivers fifty thousand volts," bragged the fatty. "Open-air arc. Twelve hundred to the body."

"There is no other stash," said Terry. "Regrettably."

"You know, kid," said the governor pensively, "I may be starting to believe it."

"Listen," said Terry, and knelt down politely in front of them. That part was improv. We never told him to kneel. "The parents *are* assholes. Morons. *We* know it. Why do you think we ran away? They're living in a fantasy. But we have something real to offer."

"As good as food?" asked the governor.

"Maybe better," said Terry.

"Shoot, then," said the governor.

"You saw their cars, right?" said Terry. "The Mercedes, the Volvo SUV, and the old Model S?"

"Yeah," said the governor. "Crap clearance, but good resale. We'll be taking those."

"Of course," said Terry. "We'd expect nothing less."

The fatties laughed. The governor smiled.

"I only mention the cars," said Terry, "for what they indicate. And what we can give you, if you promise to leave."

"What's that, kid?"

"Their money."

This was met with silence. But interest.

Our parents weren't the yacht parents. Not by a long shot. But they did have some resources.

"Is that right," said the governor slowly.

"We can get access to the bank accounts," said Rafe. "We

have a guy who's a techie. A hacker, basically. And their lap-tops. Also a mobile hotspot, if we get up on a hill near here where we happen to know there's a cell tower. If you agree to leave, we'll transfer the cash to you."

Silence again.

"Huh," said the governor. He was nodding slowly. "How much are we talking?"

"We don't have the exact figures yet," said Terry. "But we'll find out. There are some ETFs, sir. And money-market funds."

"Huh," said the governor again. Waffling.

"Worth a shot," said one of the fat ones.

"OK, kid. Give us a few minutes. We'll, uh. Take this into consideration."

He seemed sleepy. His eyes were slits.

Very stoned, I realized.

"All we ask," said Terry. "And thank you."

"You really went all out," said Rafe, when we were down the ladder again. "With the ass-kissing."

"They're not the sharpest knives in the drawer," said Terry. "I had to make it obvious."

"Mission accomplished," I said.

"Now we wait," said Rafe.

THE CROSSBOW MAN didn't seem to care what we did. I took off with a hoodie and a headlamp to check on Jack. The rain had let up a bit.

When I found him and Shel and the rest, sitting under a tarp stretched over the lean-to they'd built, the redhead was with them. Not carrying his gun anymore: Jen was holding it.

His leg was bandaged with cloth, and he was eating from a bowl, using his fingers as scoops.

"That's a pretty nice way to treat the kid who killed the best goat ever," I said to Jack.

"He was hungry," said Jack. "And thirsty. And his leg hurts a lot. So we let him toss his gun up. And then we pulled him out."

"I like macaroni," said the kid, mouth full.

"He was pretty much starving," said Jen.

"Against the Geneva Convention," said Low.

"Plus he's a mental defective," said Juicy. It wasn't quiet, but if the redhead heard he didn't voice an objection.

Jack tugged at the sleeve of my hoodie to pull me aside.

"Evie, we want to come back," he said. "Jen said the parents are here. Are they going to fix it all, Evie?"

"I don't know, Jack," I said. "Not so far. So far they've only made it worse."

"Everything's wet. And I'm so cold," he said. He wasn't exaggerating: his lips were blue and his hands were trembling. "The stove fuel's gone. And our water containers are just catching rain. Plus I *miss* you."

"But those men are dangerous," I told him. "It's not worth getting shot, is it?"

"And Red needs a doctor."

"Red? Now you're friends with him?"

"Not *friends*. Just, someone has to fix his leg. Shel says he'll always walk wrong if it doesn't get fixed. He needs help."

"He should have thought of that before he held me at gunpoint," I said.

"He doesn't think so good. He wouldn't have *shot* you."

"How do you know that, Jack? Maybe he would have shot *you*. You saw what happened to Dilly."

"Shel wrapped his leg up in his shirt. But you should see it. It looks bad under there."

I sent him back to the campfire and consulted with Jen. We weren't sure how to proceed. The soldiers seemed to be sticking to the barn and cottage. The governor was stoned and pretty out of it. For now, at least.

And the silo, at least, was warm and dry.

Maybe the little boys would be just as safe there.

Red was the wild card, said Jen. Would he throw in his lot with the soldiers again? Get us into deep shit over the leg?

"Hey, Red," I said. "Is one of the men back there your father?"

Red was licking out his bowl. He shook his head.

"Don't have a father."

"So how do you know them?"

"Work at the restaurant."

"The restaurant?"

"McDonald's," explained Jack.

"I clean there. They came there in the trucks. I let them in," said Red. "They have the keys now. They're the boss."

"I see," I said.

And I did.

BUT WHEN WE emerged from the trees we saw bright light over the field. We stopped and stared. It had been a while since we'd seen lights so bright. Blinding. They got brighter and nearer fast, lower and lower, and there was loud noise. It was the noise of a rotor.

A helicopter.

"They must have called the cops!" shouted Juice.

"*Is* it the cops?" shouted Rafe.

We had to give up shouting over the noise. Had the parents brought firepower after all? We couldn't believe it.

We saw no signs of movement around the barn.

The governor was asleep at the wheel.

We grinned at each other. I felt the madness of hope. A crazy uplift. Everyone felt it. It was contagious.

The blades whipped up a wind, and our hair blew around as the lights descended. We huddled in the wet and dark. Then it landed. It looked huge.

Men jumped out onto the grass. Guys in black, like a SWAT team. They had their own guns. They rushed toward the barn with those guns at their shoulders, in formation. They clearly had a game plan.

The chopper's blades whirred to a halt. We went toward it.

A figure in a long coat and tall boots stepped out last. A

woman. In the light I saw her face was calm. She was slight and old.

She glanced at us. Beckoned. And started to walk away.

"There are kids in the barn with the soldiers," I called out to her back, following her as the noise and lights faded behind us. "A baby. Our parents. And the trail angels and Burl. They haven't done anything wrong."

"I know," I think was what she said.

I couldn't be sure, because she didn't turn around. Her words soared out ahead of her.

SHE REACHED THE silo and we followed her in. Crossed the room at a businesslike pace and sat herself down in one of the two armchairs.

David, bent over in the other chair tapping on a laptop, uncurled himself. His face was a question.

"Are you the owner?" asked Jen.

The woman barely nodded. She slipped a phone from her coat pocket and hit a button. "Clear out the civilians," she said into it. "Put the parents in the cottage. And send the children to me." Then she slipped out a pack of cigarettes and a lighter. Lit one up, took a drag on it.

My impulse was to say she shouldn't smoke in here, but I kept my mouth shut.

"What's gonna happen to those guys?" asked Juicy.

"Well," said the owner. "I'm afraid they broke the rules."

"Noise on the weekend," ventured Jack. He stood beside me, still wet and shaking.

"That's right, dear," said the owner. Maybe I was inventing it, but I thought her expression was tender. "Among others. Go over there by the space heater, Jack. You're freezing."

Had I said his name? When?

She made some quick gestures to Shel, who stepped over to the heater too. Bent down and held his hands close to it.

That elderly woman knew her sign language.

"The rest of you. Remain," she said.

She had a way about her. I didn't consider disobeying.

"You can go upstairs if you wish," she went on. "I know you like the view. But not outside. First, bring me an ashtray, Eve."

I hadn't told her my name either.

"I don't know where—"

She waved her arm at the wall shelving. Sure enough, a small metal bowl. I placed it on the arm of her chair.

Behind us Sukey came in the door with her baby. Then Dee. They stood there shyly, waiting.

"Good," said the woman. "Let the games begin."

She hit another button on her phone.

We didn't know what she meant by that, but she wasn't saying more. She tapped her ash into the bowl. We started up the stairs.

From the platform, we gazed down at the barn. It was silent and mostly dark at first. Through one of the two windows we could see a flicker.

"Hell of a candle," said Rafe.

"They shouldn't light candles in there," said Jen.

Fog drifted into the beams of our headlamps. Someone's yell broke the silence, and we saw one of the SWAT guys silhouetted at the hay door. I could tell by his headgear and the bulky belt around his waist. His back was to us, but it looked like he had his rifle lifted.

"What's he doing?" asked Jen.

We gazed. There was more shouting. I glanced over at the cottage, whose lights were on. Its door stood open. Fathers and mothers were rushing across the grass. And filing in. I counted: eight. All of them.

A donkey walked in a leisurely way over some flagstones beside the parked cars. Clip-clop. Clip-clop.

"Seriously," said Jen. "What's he doing?"

"Guarding?" said Rafe.

Presently we heard a crackle. We saw flames leap inside one window. Then the other.

It wasn't fog, I realized.

"Tell her!" said Jen. "Tell her the barn's burning!"

So I ran down the stairs again, Juicy clattering behind me. He liked to be in on the action, Juice did.

"Your barn!" I said to the owner, breathless. "It caught on fire! The barn's burning!"

"That old thing," she said. "Not up to code. Should already have been condemned."

Still calm. Completely calm.

"But—but—"

"People are maybe stuck inside," Jack told her gravely.

"They shouldn't have played with Tasers, then," she said.

We stared at her. At least, I did.

"Or guns. Even worse. Against the rules."

"Maybe they didn't *know* the rules," said Jack.

"Of course they did, little one," said the owner. "*Everyone* knows the rules."

WE LOST A good ten minutes. Had no idea what to do. Alarmed but also paralyzed. The flames were inside the barn at first, and then they were leaping from the far side of the roof. SWAT guys filled the hay door, their backs lined up, shoulder to shoulder. A wall of dark men.

One of the barn's two windows crashed open from inside, and someone was trying to squirm out of it, but then he fell back. And flames were at the window.

That was when we knew we had to try. What if the angels were still in there?

She'd said to move the parents. And the kids. But she hadn't mentioned the angels.

We rappelled down, so that we didn't have to face the owner and the little boys would stay put. We tried the barn's double doors, but they must have been chained on the inside—we pulled and pulled but could only open them about two inches.

Putting the fire out was a losing battle. We ferried buckets back and forth from a spigot, but it wasn't helping. We tried to use the hose from the vegetable garden, but it didn't reach.

So we got rakes and shovels and started trying to bash a hole in the double doors. The smoke was thick, and we were coughing, and it was hard to see. Parents streamed out of the cottage behind us, yelling at us to get away. Shouting that the building could collapse.

Some of them pulled at us finally, physically grabbed us and tackled us to the ground and dragged—Low met this fate, and Jen—and presently the SWAT guys were there too, and we were outnumbered.

There was a shot, which we could barely hear over the noise of the fire. Then more shots, rat-tat-tat, and various parents were crying and grabbing us.

As we got forced away from the barn doors—we'd made a couple of long, ragged rents in them—the rain picked up and thunder sounded, and soon it was pouring.

The SWAT guys herded us into the cottage, where it felt like there was no room for another body to stand. Mothers and fathers were all around.

We were crowded into that kitchen like too many people in an elevator. Even the bathroom and the bedroom. We filled up the small house.

"You're safe," said a SWAT guy, but then he stepped back. Dammit if he didn't lock us in.

His voice came muffled from outside. "Just stay put now. I mean it."

INSIDE THE COTTAGE the night got long and fuzzy. We dozed fitfully crushed into each other, heaps of us upright or sitting on the floor against standing legs. Juicy and Dee curled up on the kitchen table, and I envied them.

We were damp and black with smoke and ash, and various fathers muttered and snored. Various mothers sniveled and whispered. I worried about Jack out in the silo. I don't remember how I got to sleep, but I must have, because gradually it was morning.

Light came filtering in and I realized the rain had stopped. We felt caged in and frustrated. Someone was talking about the broken bathroom window, and who was small enough to fit through it, when Juicy pushed Rafe against the inside of the door.

And discovered it was unlocked, because it opened.

Jack stood on the other side with Shel behind him. Sukey and the baby and Dee.

Also, Red. He shifted from foot to foot.

I hugged Jack really hard. I admit it.

Behind them, the barn was smoldering. No flames. It was still there, but mostly turned from red to black, and parts of it were caved in.

We ran out toward the field, but the helicopter was gone. Donkeys grazed on the flattened grass where it had been. And one goat.

There was one goat left. The soldiers had missed it.

We raced back to the cars. Our parents' were still there, but the soldiers' Jeeps were not. The gate was standing open.

Parents milled around in the front of the cottage and inside it, trying to get signals on their phone. Washing their faces and hands at the sinks. Some using the toilet, repulsively leaving the bathroom door open.

"Where are the angels?" I asked Jack. "Where's Burl?"

He shook his head. He didn't know.

"We went to sleep," he said. "Beside the heaters. That lady was nice. She made us hot chocolate on a little stove and sat there in her chair smiling. She told us stories in sign language. So Shel could listen too. Then we fell asleep. When we woke up she wasn't there."

MY MOTHER ASKED if there was a good cell signal in the neighborhood. They couldn't get one here, she said—not for voice calls. We said yeah, we had noticed.

She said they had to call the cops. The Fire Department. Everyone.

The parents still believed in Emergency Services.

Val said she knew where a cell tower was. It wouldn't do any good, but she'd lead them to it. If they insisted.

"WE HAVE TO check the barn," said Jen, after most of the parents had set out with Val. She and Sukey sat at the picnic table, Sukey giving a bottle to the baby.

The parents had zero interest in the barn. They'd let the authorities deal with it, they said.

We were outright scared to go in. The walls or roof might fall on us. And what would we discover? Would we find angels' bodies?

"One side's wide open," said David. "No roof on it anymore. We can probably walk in that part safely."

I didn't want to. At all. None of us did.

But we had to.

I made Jack and Shel wait outside, and Sukey handed Jack the baby. The rest of us stepped carefully through the ashes and burnt wood. We didn't go where flaps of roof hung down. We stayed away from the fragile walls. Everything smelled like smoke. There were no stalls anymore.

Posts and beams had fallen, and inside it was dark and hard to figure. Pieces of wall and roof shingles and planks of wood with nails in them. They had all turned black in the fire, and we couldn't tell what was what.

Then Juicy found melted guns, snarled in a pile beneath the fallen planks of the hayloft. He found some zippers from our sleeping bags.

David found the melted sole of a boot, attached to a steel toe.

Jen found a skull. With skin and hair on it.

Right away she threw up. Jen has an active gag reflex.

It wasn't Darla's hair, said Low. Or any of the angels'. It was gray. And buzzed short.

More like the governor's.

There were other bones too, ribs and big bones like leg bones. Femurs, said Juicy.

We didn't try to count the bones or make them into people. We just went out.

We left the barn. And never went back in.

A COUPLE OF fathers had stayed behind to tinker with the cars. One of the ones we'd driven wouldn't start, I guess. I went into the kitchen and turned on my phone.

On it I saw a few old, missed calls from my parents.

And a single new text from an Unknown Number.

It lifted a weight from me.

This is the owner. Don't worry about Burl and the angels, it said. *They are with me now.*

"Hey. Come here," called Jack, from outside. "Evie. The tree! Come see!"

I stepped out the door and turned around to look where he was looking. The skeleton of the dogwood, stripped of its leaves, had small white nubs all over the thinner parts of its branches. Hundreds. Thousands.

At first I thought, Disease. Fungus.

But then I realized they were the buds of flowers. It was fall, but the tree was covered in buds.

9

OUR BEDDING AND most of our clothes had burned, so we didn't have many possessions anymore. Our phones and a few clothes that had been in the cottage laundry pile. Some worn-out toothbrushes and camping items.

The parents said the roads were clearing, and some gas stations had reopened.

But who would feed the donkeys when we were gone? Jack asked them. And the lone goat that had survived? He and Shel had kept it in the woods during the shooting, he told me. Held onto its collar while the others went into the field.

The parents couldn't have cared less.

Before we left, Sukey said, she had to show them her mother's grave.

They'd been told of the death when they were given blood—David had broken the news—but some of them had been too sick to hear, and others must have been drunk. Or distracted. They hadn't even mentioned it.

Sukey wanted to make it real to them. She wanted it to hit home.

We walked in silence to the cairn in the field's corner, where the forest began. The parents kept quiet, trudging along beside us, though Jen's mother tried to reach out for her hand. She slapped the hand away.

Sukey had built the pile of rocks up to the height of a person. It was as though the cairn was a sentry. Watchful.

The stones didn't move, sure, no. But something in their posture made you think they might.

"Do you blame *us?*" asked a mother. Pathetic-sounding.

"We blame you for everything," Jen said evenly.

"Who else is there to blame?" added Rafe.

"I don't blame you," said Sukey. The baby squawked, and she jiggled it.

The mother looked at her gratefully.

"You were just stupid," said Sukey. "And lazy."

Not so grateful.

"You gave up the world," said David.

"You let them turn it all to shit," said Low.

I almost forgot the taste of old banana, then.

"I hate to disappoint you, but we don't have that much power," said a father.

"Yeah. And that's what they all said," said Jen.

"Listen. We know we let you down," said a mother. "But what could we have *done*, really?"

"Fight," said Rafe. "Did you ever fight?"

"Or did you just do exactly what you wanted?" said Jen. "Always?"

The mothers looked at each other. A father rubbed his beard. Others put hands in pockets, rocked back and forth on their heels and studied the pile of dirt beside the stones.

"So. There was a *cremation*," said a mother. Changing the subject.

"A funeral pyre," said Rafe.

"Sukey made the cairn," I said.

"It's a very strong piece," said my father, the artist.

Sukey rolled her eyes.

She could still do that, at least.

"We should say some words," said a mother.

"No you shouldn't," said Sukey.

"A benediction," said another mother.

"We already had the funeral," said Rafe.

"We sang a hymn," I said. "Well. Someone did."

"An angel," said Juicy.

He turned and spat. It hit a father's shoe.

"That's disgusting," said a mother. His.

"Good," said Juicy.

BACK AT THE buildings Jack was nowhere to be seen. Neither was Shel, and neither were the donkeys and goat.

I guessed the little boys were walking the animals to the neighbors' farm. It would make sense. Jack was following his own lights these days.

Juicy and Low took the all-terrain vehicles for a final spin across the field. Racing.

In the kitchen a mother was absentmindedly tidying. As though the cottage was a rental, and we had to leave it clean.

"I don't think the cops are coming," said a father, from the bathroom.

"You don't say," said Rafe.

"We have to wait for Jack and Shel," I told my own mother.

She'd found a can of beer at the back of the fridge, and was popping the tab.

"Do you have somewhere to go, dear?" she asked.

Addressing Red, who sat at the table gnawing the dirt out of his fingernails. He'd picked up one of the useless, melted guns and stuck it into the ammo belt he wore.

Must have thought it looked dashing.

He shook his head.

"A home?" she prodded.

"Don't have one," said Red.

It was then I noticed his leg wasn't wrapped up. And I realized he'd been walking normally all day.

"Wait," I said. "Your leg. You said it was broken. Is it just a sprain?"

I was exasperated. Jack had said he wouldn't walk right, and we'd been ready to risk our own skins.

"It *was* broken. She fixed it," said Red.

"She set your leg? The owner set your leg?" asked Jen.

He shrugged. "She fixed it."

He hiked up a pant. We saw a regular skinny, hairy leg. Just nothing wrong with it.

"Wait," said Jen. "I saw that thing. Even a doctor . . ."

She looked at me. Shook her head. Baffled.

I'd never seen the injury myself, so I had no opinion.

"She told me to stay here," said Red.

"Who told you?" asked Jen.

"*She,*" said Red. "Owner. Said I'm the new caretaker."

"*You?*" asked Rafe.

"She put my finger on the pad," said Red.

He didn't have a home. So the owner had given him one.

THE PARENTS' AGENDA was basically what ours had been: the shelter of wealth. We would strike out for Juicy's mansion.

His family was still the richest.

"Do you think it might have worked?" I asked David, as he and Rafe and I stood at the field's edge waiting for the little boys. "The plan to give the soldiers their money?"

"Maybe," he said. "Depends how strong the security sys-

tems were on the other laptops. I'd just cracked my parents'
when the barn-burning went down. Not much cash there.
That one was gonna be a wash."

"We gave it the old college try," said Rafe. "The diplo-
mat's path. A peaceful solution."

"Wouldn't have been peaceful later," I said.

"True dat," said David.

We grinned at each other, imagining the parents' rage.
Besides drinking, money was the one thing they were dead
serious about.

"Evie!" called Jack. "The neighbors were home! They're
really nice. They're going to take care of the donkeys. And
Jiminy."

Shel nodded.

"We have to go now, Jack," I said. "It's time."

"I know, Evie," he said.

WE HAD SIX cars including the van, so we had to crowd in.
Jen and Shel rode in our car.

Jack had run around looking for his barn owl to say
goodbye, but the owl must have been sleeping somewhere.
He cried a little when he couldn't find it, and Shel was
down too. They sat close together, moping. Jen squeezed in
beside me.

As the caravan pulled out Red watched us go from the
top of the silo. Waved his melted gun in a rough salute.

I FELT LIKE a refugee. Or a prisoner of war. Possibly both.

My mother got on her phone as soon as she had a signal, talking logistics. Where to stop for gas and food. Where the safe zones were. She mentioned the National Guard, and something about checkpoints.

Jen and I stared out the window.

It wasn't how we remembered. There were power lines down everywhere, and piles of fallen trees and branches shoved out of the way along the roads. There were brown rivers in ditches, with piles of garbage. People straggled along in small groups beside the road. There were abandoned cars, a jackknifed semi. Dark storefronts with doors standing open. There were roadkilled dogs and birds and rabbits and raccoons, even some deer.

There was more roadkill than I'd ever seen.

"Keep the windows up," my mother said. "The *smell!*"

Armies of creatures had gone to battle on those roads. But they hadn't known. No one had told them it was war.

Crows and vultures lit up from the carcasses.

Maybe that many had always gotten hit, said Jen. But now no one was here to take away their bodies.

After Jack saw the first dead animals he got tears in his eyes. Stopped looking outside. He and Shel stared down at games on their tablets, where bright palaces stood on green hills.

Through the glass we saw signs of life: workmen ran around carrying loops of cables and shouldering ladders, yelling over their shoulders. We passed road crews wearing hi-vis jackets and hardhats. We passed a crane and linemen working on a utility pole. We passed other families in their cars, which were crowded like ours.

Children gazed back at us from their own rear windows.

The land had a different texture. Old and tired. Almost derelict.

WHEN WE STOPPED for gas it was all of our cars at once. The parents didn't want to risk a separation. Men held up signs at the curb, GAS HERE. And NO CREDIT.

We pulled up to a pump in two rows. Only those who had to pee were allowed out, so I said I had to pee. Jen said she did too.

"Leave your phones in the car," said my father.

He didn't trust us, I guess.

Which was fair. We didn't trust him either.

"Five minutes is all you get," he said.

So we went to the bathroom for something to do. But it was filthy, with clogged toilets and clumps of soaked paper and soiled diapers on the floor, and we didn't even care to use the sink. Instead we hung around in the mini-mart looking at the empty shelves. They were mostly empty. Still left were pork rinds, limón and chile flavor. Two rolls of breath mints.

At the cash register a very old clerk, his face like a fossil, watched us suspiciously. Maybe thought we were thieves.

"Tampons!" said Jen.

They were behind the counter with the chewing tobacco.

"How much for a box?" I asked the clerk, pointing. Out of curiosity. We had no money of our own.

"Forty."

"Cents?"

"Dollars."

"*Forty*," whispered Jen as we left.

As WE GOT close to Juicy's neighborhood the streets were cleaner, the piles of dead animals tapered off, and there were more crews fixing the phones and electricity. Around us mansions were set back from the road, with elaborate landscaping. Massive rolling lawns had been mowed. Garbage had been collected.

"The other half," said Jen.

"*We're* the other half," I said.

"At least for now."

"It's all for now," said Jack.

He sounded eighty-three.

We pulled up behind the other cars at some tall metal gates. An initial in metal script at the top, tacky. We sat there waiting for the gates to open.

"Look! See? The promised land," I said to Jack, and nudged him to glance up from his tablet.

"We already *had* the promised land, Evie," he said softly.

"Hey, Jack," said my father, trying to catch his eye in the

rearview mirror. Summoned a smile that looked fake. And a jocular tone. "Chin up, kid. Everything's going to be OK!"

Jack switched his tablet off and flipped it over. Rested his hands on it, neatly folded together.

"That's what you always said," he said. His voice was still soft. "You're my father. But you're a *liar*."

From the front seat there was only silence.

GOING UP THE long drive, we passed resplendent flowerbeds with purple-cabbage borders, abstract-sculpture fountains spouting clear water, groves of trees already turning yellow and red.

Jen whistled between her teeth.

"Not too shabby," said my father.

"All this from a few shitty movies," said my mother.

"They're not all shitty."

"Most of them. He says so himself."

"You should see the spread in Bel Air," said my father.

"*You* haven't seen it," retorted my mother.

"Have too. On social media."

She snorted.

We parked. There was a shaded parking lot. I could see a lacy gazebo in the distance, and through some trees part of a giant, frilly white house that looked like a fake version of someplace in Europe. Maybe Italy.

"I'm going straight into the pool," said my mother, unclipping her seatbelt. "And then the Jacuzzi. I hear it's got a glass roof on it."

"How can you have an infinity pool without an ocean?" asked Jen.

"I guess we'll find out," said my father.

"The bar had better be well stocked," said my mother.

And got out.

"*She's* not entitled," muttered Jen.

WE CHOSE THE guesthouse for ourselves, for the sake of privacy. Except for Dee, who elected to share the servants' quarters in fake Italy with the bratty twins. And Juicy, who wanted to sleep in his own bedroom.

The parents who hadn't come to the farm had got to the mansion first, and one of them had been sleeping in Juicy's bed and had to be ejected.

But living in the main house didn't mean he'd hang out with the 'rents, he assured us. Fuck that.

We gave him a pass.

The guesthouse only had three bedrooms, but there was also a living room with a pullout bed in the couch. There were three other couches, one of them L-shaped. There was a small kitchen and two bathrooms. We let Sukey and Jen have a bedroom for themselves and the baby, so when the baby cried there'd be a door we could close.

Then we got warm, and dry, and clean.

"They tried to confiscate her on the way here," Sukey told us, when we were setting up our sleeping arrangements.

"Confiscate? The baby?"

"They said they had to take care of her. That I'm too young for the responsibility."

It sounded like a vacation to me.

"I said no fucking way," said Sukey.

"I mean, you could use them for babysitting sometimes," suggested Jen.

"Hmph," said Sukey.

FOR A SHORT while the days passed in that place as they might in a fairy-tale castle. For a while there were even servants—a housekeeper and cleaning team, gardeners, a pet groomer for the dogs. They came and went.

In the great house we'd been blissfully ignored, on the farm we'd been left to ourselves. Here, at first, we lived a mostly separate life. Juicy's parents gave us clothes from their walk-in closets, each bigger than my room at home had been. And we had a budget for online shopping: Terry made a modest proposal and the parents accepted. We even ordered our own groceries.

There was no budget for alcohol or weed, obviously. Those still had to be pilfered. But Juicy knew the ropes—been doing it for years.

There were new rules on tech and the Internet, rules the

parents imposed on themselves. One hour of news at night, one hour in the morning. At other times, they shut down the Wi-Fi and turned off the TVs. And they quarantined not our phones, but their own. It was unhealthy to wallow in everyone else's misery, one mother said.

They made exceptions for money and work. The fathers said they had to watch their investments, and a few parents were still employed in some form. Part-time. A couple of professors were teaching online courses, including my mother, who said feminist theory didn't rest.

But yeah, she admitted. Enrollment was way down.

Other than that, they followed their usual routine. At breakfast, Bloody Marys and Irish coffees. Beer at lunch, and when the clock hit four, open season.

JACK WAS POLITE to our parents. Polite but distant. He'd trusted them once, but they had let him down. I got the feeling he was trying to muster some of his old, faithful affection for them and not having much success. They were unreliable sources.

Myself, I'd never expected much. Not since I was even younger than him, anyway. I'd stopped holding their hands when I was seven. And never done it again. I remember the last time clearly: we'd passed a large crowd in a square in Manhattan. Union Square, I deduced later. The crowd was pissed. Shouting protests. Waving signs. I don't know what they said—I was too short to read them. Between my parents, each of my hands in one of theirs, I asked them why.

It doesn't matter, they said. I pestered them. I wouldn't let it go. *They* could read the signs. They were tall enough.

But they flatly refused to tell me. Be quiet, they said. They were late for a dinner appointment. Reservations at that place were *impossible* to get. I wrenched my hands out of theirs. Ran into the crowd, weaving between strangers' legs. Tugging on the arms of people's jackets. Asking them why they were so mad. A couple answered, but I couldn't hear what they said.

My father chased me and finally caught up. His face red and sweaty and his teeth gritted. Now they were *very* late, thanks to me, he said. I was grounded.

Lately, whenever I felt a surge of resentment, I reminded myself of the recognition I'd had after I ate the moldy bread.

Because my mother and my father—they weren't so different from Red. They'd functioned passably in a limited domain. Specifically adapted to life in their own small niches. Habitat specialists, Mattie might have said.

My father's habitat had been the art economy. He'd moved there with ease, making and selling his looming, colorful sculptures of war-torn women. He'd known how to navigate receptions at galleries and museums, offer up to collectors and critics his offhand ironic pronouncements and eccentric behavior. Garnered six-figure payouts for the voluptuous breasts he'd covered with scenes of destruction from Afghanistan and Syria and Yemen. The asses that bore images of bombed-out homes and burning hospitals.

My mother's habitat had been the university, her articles full of long words and the names of other scholars. Articles five people read.

When their habitats collapsed they had no familiar terrain. No map. No equipment. No tools.

Just some melted guns strapped to their waists.

BY AND BY we found ourselves getting bored. There was only so much cold-weather swimming to be done in the solar-heated infinity pool (a cascade of basins on a hillside, getting smaller and smaller as you progressed down the slope). There was a three-hole golf course, a volleyball pit, and even an indoor squash court in fake Italy's basement, along with a small bowling alley.

Our interest in these pastimes waxed and waned. We started to learn sign language, co-taught by Jack and Shel. A little Spanish from Sukey. Jen let Terry sleep in her bed with her, and I even implied to Low I might make out with him the day he learned to dress. And regularly brush his teeth.

Right away he started borrowing clothes from Rafe. The pants were too short and his ankles stuck out of them.

Still. Maybe I'd cut him some slack.

TERRY PROPOSED A new game: we'd meet the parents before dinner and play in teams, us vs. the elderly. The team that won could claim a prize from the other.

Whatever prize they chose, within reason.

"But what can we give *them*?" asked Rafe.

"Our time, maybe," said Sukey.

"Our labor," said David.

"Bartending services," said Juice, who was teaching himself mixology.

"They'd have to give us booze, if we demanded," said Jen. "Let's face it, props to Juice, but stealing doesn't always cut it."

"More *is* better," said Juice.

"More's better, typically," agreed Val.

She didn't drink, herself. She'd been melancholy without Burl but refused to self-medicate. No booze, no weed, and no evidence of libido either. Val was a straight edge all the way.

Or she hadn't hit puberty. We didn't know which.

So we told them what the game was—a simple one we used to play on road trips. One person thought of a word or phrase, and the other team had to guess it by asking a series of questions. The word could be a person, place, thing, or concept.

In some of these domains the elderly had a clear strategic advantage. Many of them, frankly, knew more facts. Plus they'd had professional development in their fields.

They agreed to the reward system, confident of victory.

But we had screens, we had time, and we were looking for a challenge. When each afternoon rolled around we set ourselves to learning. There were trivia websites, and those could be useful. There was Wikipedia. We crammed.

The first game ended in our defeat when the parents won three words running thinking of the names Bella Abzug, Christine de Pizan, and Margery Kempe. They crowed in jubilation and claimed eight hours of "tech advice" from David, which was what they called it when he performed fixes and workarounds for them.

"Advice" implied a back-and-forth, but they didn't want to understand. They just wanted service.

As a reward for David, Juicy procured three full lines of his mother's excellent cocaine. That was risky for Juice, since his mother monitored her coke stash like a harpy eagle with newborn chicks.

David was duly grateful.

The second game we lost as badly as the first. They made Sukey hand over her sister for a day, so they could "have some cute baby time" (gag). She protested, but we decided the prize was probably legit. Sukey submitted to the majority, then paced back and forth most of that day, worrying the parents would wreck the baby.

Her sister was barely two months old, said Jen. How much damage could they actually do?

Sukey retorted that they couldn't be trusted with child-rearing. On that front we had to agree.

When the infant was returned, swaddled and diapered and fed, she looked and acted exactly the same, of course—lay there without doing anything, occasionally crying—but Sukey was still suspicious. They'd put a dumb-looking pink bow on her head, which Sukey ripped off with extreme prejudice.

In the third game the parents were drunker than usual, and arrogant. It ended in a draw requiring a tiebreaker. The elderly could barely believe it: we stymied them with Nicki Minaj, which would have been a shoo-in for us.

"And she's a feminist," I told my mother, sticking the knife in.

"Debatable," said my mother, googling.

We took home beer and liquor.

OVER TIME, THOUGH, a new darkness settled on them. Crashing stock markets were a factor, and weather. It wasn't storming where we were, but there were many storms elsewhere. Also droughts and heat waves. Cold and hot fronts, defunct trade routes. Everywhere seemed to be in flux. The weather shut down airports, and ruined crops were "destabilizing" the markets. The North Pole was far too warm. Parts of Europe were freezing.

Plus the domestic staff had quit.

The parents complained, indignant. It was so sudden, they said. They'd all been told there was more time. *Way* more. It was someone else's fault, that was for sure. Not the scientists, said one. Those guys had tried their best. Maybe the politicians. And possibly the journalists.

We heard discussions about hoarding, and the pros and cons of stockpiling different commodities. What would the best currency be? The parents talked about this for hours on end. For a while it was their obsession.

Gold? Weapons? Ammunition? Batteries? Antibiotics? Arguments transpired, and we perceived unrest. Disputes and resolutions.

But no consensus. A diverse portfolio was safest, they decided.

So shipments arrived constantly. There were solar panels and dry goods and medicines. Sometimes the parents spent days unpacking them. Phrases like "disease migration" and "parasites" were bandied about, and trucks arrived loaded with bottled water. Not spring water in small bottles—oh no. Water in large barrels, water they stored in a corrugated-metal warehouse that workers had constructed while we were living in the great house.

Men came out to beef up the security system. And build. Where once the fence along the mansion's perimeter had been a wrought-iron decoration, now it was a concrete wall fortified with electrical charges. There were booby traps at the base of the wall, and no-fly zones. The no-fly zones were no-walk zones, in fact, but the parents called them no-fly zones, and we took their meaning. Construction workers walked the perimeter and set things into the ground, then built a fence inside the main wall as a buffer. We weren't permitted to touch it.

"Land mines?" asked Juicy.

"Can't be. Illegal," said Rafe.

But we weren't convinced. We didn't think of stepping onto that grass. We never let the dogs off-leash.

AFTER THE WALL was built we held them to the game harder than ever. They needed the ritual to feel normal, was what we didn't say but knew.

We were winning more and more, and the parents got so discouraged that now and then we lost to them on purpose. We'd pick an easy guess. "The rings of Saturn," one of us might choose to think, or "naked mole rat" or even "cauliflower."

The game might be interrupted by a parent getting a text from a friend or relative. When it began we'd had a strict attitude about such interruptions, not wanting a losing contender to cheat via search engine. But when a mother got weepy or a father white-faced over what they read in a text, increasingly we let it go.

One father wandered off the property—Jen's—and when he came back was pretty much catatonic. He was missing his shoes, and his bare feet were bloody and frostbitten. He wouldn't say what had happened. He squatted in the kitchen of fake Italy and rocked back and forth, his arms around his knees.

A mother went on a Skype bender, though connectivity was spotty. She looked up all the friends and family she'd ever had. The ones she couldn't raise she made a list of and tried to track down by other means. The ones she *could* get hold of were almost worse. A few were maybe all right, others were panicked or seemed to be in a state of stunned confusion. Two asked to come live with us, and the mother appealed, begging, to Juicy's father.

"No way," he said. "You know we discussed this."

"Don't do this to yourself," said my mother, always practical. "All we can do is cultivate our garden."

We didn't get that, until, cramming, we came across it in the famous sayings of a dead Frenchman.

At times a parent would forget to eat for several meals running. Some of them let themselves get dirty and began to smell. Some floated in the pool on blow-up rafts for hours, even though it was cold outside, listening to music and speaking to nobody. One threw a tantrum and smashed her bathroom mirror with a crowbar.

We called a meeting.

"If this is where we're going to stay, we have to whip it into shape," said Rafe.

"Someone has got to get things organized," said Jen. "It can't go on like this."

"And we can't depend so much on the outside," said Sukey. "Supplies from there are dwindling."

"We're going to need to take over," said David.

WE TALKED ABOUT growing our own food, but winter was upon us so we discussed research Low and Rafe had been conducting on the how-tos of hydroponics. We decided the hot-tub building, with its glass walls and roof, could be repurposed. We talked about seeds, the availability of crop plants and grow lamps, the generators and the solar array. Whether David could figure out how to take us off the intermittently failing grid, with its brownouts and blackouts, and wire us up to be a closed system.

That was a tough brief, but he was cautiously optimistic. We talked about skills and divisions of labor.

One night, instead of playing the game, we called the parents to order.

"It's come to our attention," said Terry, who'd ordered new glasses and restored his grandiosity along with his vision, "that many of you are not doing so well. Let me be clear. What I mean is, psychologically."

The parents shifted in their seats. Looks passed between them, less skeptical than guilty.

"It's to be expected," he said generously. "Much as we rely on you to sustain the needs of our material existence from a financial standpoint, so you, in turn, have relied on the sociocultural order. An order that, as we all know, has recently been egregiously disrupted."

"Disrupted," echoed a mother.

"Egregiously," said Val.

"Nevertheless, your fitness to maintain order has been undermined," said Terry. "So from now until the day when your collective is restored to its baseline competency level, we'd like to take on more responsibility. We've drawn up a plan for the property's self-sufficiency, which is, of course, a work in progress. The situation and the availability of components are dynamic. We realize that. Your wealth will be of tremendous assistance, but resilience will be called for."

"Resilience," said Val.

She was standing behind Terry to one side, with her arms crossed. Seemed to relish the position.

"We've also drawn up a work schedule. In draft form currently, till we have all the information. You will continue to contribute, each in a manner appropriate to his or her abilities. Your contributions will be much appreciated. None is too small. You may be confident of that."

"A palace coup," muttered a father.

"Is Terry reading off cue cards?" asked someone in the back.

"We're also passing out a survey. We'd like you to rank your skills, in order of proficiency. This will allow us to maximize efficient task allotment."

"You're just kids," said a mother.

"But not mental defectives," said Juicy.

"And seldom drunk," said Rafe.

"Seldom," said Val.

"Our vices are our own business," said a father.

"Still, they have a point," said a mother.

"You may review the schematics and the work plan," said Terry. "Your feedback will be of special interest."

"Very charitable of you," said a father.

"Though it will *not*, of course, be treated as dispositive," added Terry.

"What skills do you want us to list? I did a class in Japanese flower-arranging," said a mother.

"Ikebana," said Terry, unswayed by her cheekiness. "I'm familiar with it. Probably not a priority."

So they took the plans under review. And the upshot was, they agreed.

Some fathers chafed, parading their superior knowledge in the realms of engineering or cash liquidity. We had to concede that not all of what they said was nonsense. We took their opinions under advisement, as Terry put it. Made modifications accordingly.

And then we started the projects.

A LONG TIME of industry followed. The parents were helpful, although they sometimes had to be encouraged. We used a bit of the carrot and a bit of the stick.

They tended to get tired as drinking and talking time rolled around, and there were instances when we had to withhold their libations until a job was completed (the stick). We weren't punitive, only firm. Juicy stooped to mockery once or twice and had to be reined in. He also stopped spitting entirely, and though he'd never let himself be called Justin—the celebrity tie-ins were too embarrassing—he did start answering to Just.

At other moments we rewarded them with extra leisure or, in front of another parent, lavish praise (the carrot). They responded to both more or less equally, in terms of what they accomplished.

Even the bratty twins pitched in. In exchange for stale candy none of the rest of us wanted, they did menial jobs like diaper washing and folding.

Were we slave drivers? asked Jen at one point.

She sometimes worried about morality.

No, said David, because we worked so hard ourselves.

And it was for everyone's benefit, said Rafe.

By late winter all the vegetables we ate were coming from the hydroponic nursery and the indoor garden in the basement (which used to be the squash court). Fresh produce could no longer be ordered online—no refrigerated trucks were running, at least not for the average rich person in our neck of the woods—so we had to eat what we grew.

We didn't have fruit, of course. We'd planted apple trees, but it'd be years before they were fruit-bearing: that planting was a Hail Mary. No citrus at all, and we missed our orange juice and lemonade. The parents missed their slices of lime.

And we had dry and canned goods, a trove far more extensive than the one in the silo. We had made sure of that.

When the day's work was done we got into the habit of preparing dinner for everyone, with the help of some mothers whose highest-rated skills were cooking. We'd all sit around in the vast sunken living room of fake Italy, with its wall of glass that opened onto the patio and the pool. We held our plates on our laps, eating and talking about the things we missed. The peasant mother was allowed to recite a blessing. Nondenominational.

She'd turned out—just as Sukey had suggested, way back when—to be no one's mother at all. All she had was the cat. But I still thought of her as the peasant one.

Then we'd go through our missings. That was what Jack called them. We figured it was healthy, for the parents especially, not to try to deny the fact of what had been lost but to acknowledge it.

Someone would mention a colleague or an ex, a grandparent or a bicycle or a neighborhood or a store. A beach or a town or a movie. Someone would say "ice cream" and someone else would say "ice-cream sandwiches, Neapolitan," and we'd riff on it, go down a list of favorite ice-cream novelties that couldn't be had anymore for love or money.

"Bars," a parent would say, and they'd rhyme off the bars they'd been to, the dive bars, the Irish bars, the cantinas. The hotel bars, the bars with jukeboxes, the bars with pool tables or views of parks and rivers. The bars that revolved. The bars at the top of glittering skyscrapers far away. In the once-great cities of the world.

10

AFTER THE SYSTEMS were in place, and the parents' tasks were complete save for basic daily upkeep, they were satisfied for a while. Proud of us all, of a job well done, for a brief period. We'd bought ourselves a good deal of time, and they knew it.

But soon enough they lapsed into a form of depression, though many of them took a cocktail of antidepressants. The pills had never done much that we could see—no doubt their effects had been dulled by alcohol—and in any case the supply was running out.

We began to detect changes, subtle at first. You might call it weakness, but I'd say it was more like absence. Their personalities were fading.

As though, if you held the parents up to the light—if

you could lift them easily, like paper—you'd be able to see right through them.

Unlike before, it wasn't an attitude we could change. It wasn't attitude at all. It was a mode of existence.

They stopped trying to entertain each other with so-called wit. They didn't talk much or laugh, even when they were drinking. And they drank less and less, shocking us. They went to bed early and slept late, saying they liked their dreams.

The dreams were the best part, one of them said.

The only part, said another.

But often their sleep was troubled. Sometimes we saw one of them out in the garden at 2 or 3 a.m. in his or her pajamas, standing or sleepwalking.

Night terrors, said Sukey. She'd read about it. You couldn't talk to them in that state.

We'd get up and throw clothes on and guide them back inside, for they never remembered to wear coats or boots and it could be below zero out there. They didn't seem to feel the cold.

For them time had turned fluid. Before we started the projects, they'd skipped meals, as I mentioned—neglected themselves. Now there were no formal meals at all except the ones we forced on them. They stuck their hands into stale bags of chips, when it occurred to them, or jars of nuts left over from the time before scarcity. Or they might gnaw on a bean or raw potato, a mushroom from the mushroom cave in the nursery.

Low's idea, and we were proud of that cave. Mushrooms grew in the dark. And they were nutritious.

Small children also suffered from night terrors, said Sukey. They *also* had a fluid sense of time. Maybe the parents were regressing.

She'd been studying up on how to raise babies. And toddlers. And five-year-olds.

No, they were just disappearing, said Rafe.

They were disappearing in plain sight.

WE CONDUCTED SOME interventions—tried to revive the game, and then board games and cards. Back in the day they used to love poker.

But they paid no attention. When they spoke, it was to tell us we could play our games without them.

"You don't need us," a mother said one evening, faint but certain.

Others nodded and went back to their dreaming.

We experimented with physical fitness, even using valuable electricity to put their old-time music on, dancing like fools to try to inspire them. It was humiliating, but we did it anyway. We figured maybe if they exercised, if they moved their bodies, life would return to them. We'd read that tip on out-of-date websites on the subject of emotional well-being.

We tried a drill-sergeant approach, forcing them to stand and walk in formation, but many of them got distracted and wandered off, then had to be corralled again.

We built an obstacle course and tried to push them through it. We injected false cheer.

We had bouts of hysteria, trying to rouse them from their lethargy. Days of exhaustion and embarrassment.

Our antics were ridiculous.

It did no good.

We felt a kind of desperation, then. For as much as we'd long felt harassed and condescended to by them, as much as we reviled them and all they'd failed to stand up for and against, we'd come to rely on their consistency.

For our whole lives, we'd been so *used* to them.

But they were slowly detaching.

ONE MORNING, WHEN we woke up, they were simply gone.

They'd left their phones, their wallets, all their personal belongings. They were nowhere on the property.

We combed the empty streets nearby, first on foot, then in the only car that still ran. The electric one.

We couldn't find them.

VAL PICTURED THE parents climbing to the tops of the tall trees that grew along the garden's edges, cedars and Lombardy poplars that were almost impossible to scale, even for her. She saw them perched on the pinnacles of those slender trees until a breeze swept in and carried them off.

Juice pictured them stepping onto the forbidden strip

of ground between the fence and the wall, vaporized one by one.

Jen saw them getting into a stretch limo and being driven off to live in a colony all their own, without the burden of children. Or even the memory.

Low saw them ride away like shepherds on the steppes, atop dark horses that appeared from nowhere. And faded into nothing the farther from us they got.

Myself, I pictured them walking down the cascading steps of the pool, their fingertips tingling. Down, down, and down, to the narrow end of infinity.

WE KEPT THEIR names on the schedules for a while, performing their assigned chores for them. We kept their bedrooms how they'd left them, until gradually we began moving in.

We labeled their phones and billfolds and purses and locked them in a cabinet in Juice's father's study, for the phones and numbers and cards and cash might one day be needed.

For some time we expected them every day. Then weekly we'd consider them, talk about how they might act when they returned. The state they might be in, injured or hungry. Whether they'd be their old selves or the changed ones.

We waited for them to come back, but they never did.

"WHAT HAPPENS AT the end?" Jack asked me.

He was sick by then, but I was going to make sure he got

better. Whenever I wasn't at his bedside, I was researching symptoms and diagnoses. How to repurpose the medicines we had. Home remedies.

I wished the angels were still with us. Luca. And Mattie. Or even the owner. Descending in her black chariot. Where was the owner when we needed her most?

Still I was dedicated. If it was the only fine thing I ever did, the single worthwhile thing, one day he'd be all right again.

"The end of what, Jack?"

"You know. The *story*. After the chaos time? It wasn't in my book. But *all* books should have a real ending."

"They should."

"She said the real end wasn't even *in* the kids' version. She said it wasn't nice. Too violent. She said that children couldn't handle relevation."

"I think she said *Revelation*."

"So what happens *after* the end?"

"Let me think. Hold on a minute. I'm thinking."

"Think better, Evie."

"OK. Slowness, I bet. New kinds of animals evolve. Some other creatures come and live here, like we did. And all the old beautiful things will still be in the air. Invisible but there. Like, I don't know. An expectation that sort of hovers. Even when we're all gone."

"But we won't be there to see them. We won't *be* here. It hurts not to know. We won't be here to see!"

He was agitated.

I held his hot hand.

"Others will, honey. Think of them. Maybe the ants. The trees and plants. Maybe the flowers will be our eyes."

"Flowers don't *have* eyes. That's like something *Darla* would say. It's not science, Evie."

"You're right. It's more like art. Poetry. But it still comes from what they used to call God, doesn't it?"

"What they used to call God," he murmured.

He was happiest when I was there talking to him, but he was getting so tired in those days. So very tired.

"You had it in your notebook, right? You wrote it down yourself, didn't you."

"I wrote it down."

"I think you solved it, Jack. In your notebook. Jesus was science. Knowing stuff. Right? And the Holy Ghost was all the things that people make. You remember? Your diagram said *making stuff.*"

"Yes. It did."

"So maybe art is the Holy Ghost. Maybe art is the ghost in the machine."

"Art is the ghost."

"The comets and the stars will be our eyes," I told him.

And I went on. The clouds the moon. The dirt the rocks the water and the wind. We call that hope, you see.

Acknowledgments

Deepest thanks to Maria Massie, my agent, and Jenny Offill, my reader. And to Aaron Young, for all the dinners he made for my children while I was writing. I'm very grateful to Tom Mayer and Elizabeth Riley, my best friends at W. W. Norton, and everyone else at Norton who helped with this book: Nneoma Amadi-Obi, Julia Reidhead, Brendan Curry, Nomi Victor, Julia Druskin, Don Rifkin, Ingsu Liu, Alexa Pugh, Steve Colca, Meredith McGinnis, Beth Steidle, and Steven Pace and his team, especially Karen Rice, Sharon Gamboa, Golda Rademacher, and Meg Sherman. Finally, thank you to David High for a beautiful cover.